Introduction 8

Introduction

A. O. Chater
Alan Coren
Ted Hughes
Jim Hunter
Jason McManus
Julian Mitchell

Introduction 2

Francis Hope
Sheila Macleod
Angus Stewart
Tom Stoppard
Garth St Omer

Introduction 3

Rachel Bush
Christopher Hampton
Michael Hoyland
Roy Watkins
John Wheway

Introduction 4

Ian Cochrane
Vincent Lawrence
Brian Phelan
Neil Rathmell
Irene Summy

Introduction 5

Adrian Kenny
Sara Maitland
David Pownall
Alick Rowe
Lorna Tracy

Introduction 6

John Abulafia
Jim Crace
Thomas Healy
Victor Kelleher
John Mackendrick

Introduction 7

Kazuo Ishiguro
J. K. Klavans
Steven Kupfer
Tim Owens
Amanda Hemingway

Introduction 8

Stories by New Writers

faber and faber

LONDON · BOSTON

First published in 1983
by Faber and Faber Limited
3 Queen Square London WC1N 3AU
Set by Wyvern Typesetting Ltd Bristol
Printed in Great Britain by
Redwood Burn Ltd Trowbridge
All rights reserved

"Passages" and "The Journey to Somewhere Else" © Anne Devlin, 1982, 1983;
"Naming the Names" © Anne Devlin, 1983

"Secrets" © Ronald Frame, 1981, 1983; "Piccadilly Peccadilloes" and "The
Tree House" © Ronald Frame, 1983

"Mrs Elizabeth Davies" © Rachel Gould, 1982, 1983; "A Private View" and
"Thucydides" © Rachel Gould, 1983

"The Lizard behind the Lavatory Cistern" © Helen Harris, 1981, 1983; "Sea
View" and "The Other Launderette" © Helen Harris, 1983

"Stunning the Punters" © Robert Sproat, 1982, 1983; "Like Some Royal King
of Honour all upon the Banks of Troy" and "Question Marks" © Robert
Sproat, 1983

Library of Congress Data has been applied for.

This book has been published with subsidy from the
Arts Council of Great Britain

British Library Cataloguing in Publication Data

Introduction.
8
1. Short stories, English
823'.01'08[FS]   PR1309.S5

ISBN 0–571–13115–8

Contents

Publisher's Note

In this collection, the eighth to appear in the INTRODUCTION series, it is our aim once again to introduce five new writers to a wider reading public. As before, the number of contributors is restricted to give each the advantage of presenting a substantial amount of work.

The INTRODUCTION series has now provided a number of well-known writers with a first chance to establish their reputations; they include Ted Hughes, Julian Mitchell, Jim Hunter, Francis Hope, Tom Stoppard, Garth St Omer, Christopher Hampton and Kazuo Ishiguro. We believe that this new collection maintains the high standard set in the past.

Biographical Notes

ANNE DEVLIN was born in Belfast in 1951. Her first play *The Long March* was broadcast on Radio 4 in November 1982. She was one of the winners of the Hennessy Literary Awards in 1982 for short stories.

RONALD FRAME was born in 1953 in Glasgow, and was educated there and at Oxford. His stories have been published widely in magazines and broadcast on the national radio.

RACHEL GOULD was born in 1955. Following an Oxford degree, she has worked for *Vogue* and has contributed articles to the *Guardian* and *The Times*. In 1982, she was a runner-up for the Catherine Pakenham award and had her first story published in *Vogue*.

HELEN HARRIS was born in 1955. She read French and Russian at Oxford and then spent a year in France. She now lives in London. Her work has appeared in many magazines and anthologies and she has just completed her first novel.

ROBERT SPROAT was born in Glasgow in 1944, was brought up in Moray and South Pembrokeshire, and has lived and worked in London since 1965.

Anne Devlin

PASSAGES
THE JOURNEY TO SOMEWHERE ELSE
NAMING THE NAMES

Passages

I have a strange story to tell. Even now it is not easy for me to remember how much I actually did hear or see, and how much I imagined. The journey between the shore of memory and the landfall of imagination is an unknown distance, because for each voyager it is a passage through a different domain. This story has a little to do with mapping that passage, but only a little: it is also a confession.

In the summer of '72 I was travelling in Ireland, calling on friends in Dublin, seeing relatives in the West, putting minor touches to my book on Dreams, looking for more folk-tales, and eavesdropping on people's dreams without drawing too much attention to the fact that it was my profession. I have been involved in analysis for several years. I'm not popular with colleagues because they see me as a kind of "pop" analyst—a collector of stories. And in a way that is what I am. On this occasion, while I was staying in Dublin at Sandycove in a house belonging to some friends who had gone abroad for a few months, a girl came to see me.

She had heard I was in Dublin, indeed she knew that I was expected to give a public lecture at Trinity that evening on the subject of my book and so she came to see me because she had a dream to tell me. This is not so strange as it sounds. I had asked several of my colleagues at the university if any of the undergraduates they taught would be prepared to volunteer unusual or disturbing dreams which might help in my research. I was not interested in individual analysis, or the concept of "cure"—I made that perfectly clear: I was interested merely in

13

the content of dream stories as a source for fiction. My earlier publication had been on 'History and the Imagination: a study of Nordic, Greek and Celtic Mythology'. My next inevitable step was to turn my attention to dream territory. I had advertised and asked for people with particularly unusual, disturbing or prophetic dreams to come forward; I had promised privacy in that I did not wish to know the identity of the people concerned.

An old college friend of mine who was teaching history at Trinity rang me on the morning the girl came to see me. He explained that one of his students had a dream to tell which she did not wish to write down but which she thought might be of interest to me. I agreed to see her at his insistence. This was the girl who came. I was more aware of the dangers of exposing dreams than most others; dreams are very confessional; they offer a power relationship to the hearer in that they ask for absolution. They are a freeing device for the speaker, but the sin has to rest with someone: the priest absolves the sin he also carries with him; like the Christ figure he carries the cross that others may be free. This was not a role I cherished or viewed with any great pleasure. I was very wary of people who did invite others to unburden themselves—the result could only be masochism or sadism: the wilful acceptance of suffering or the inflicting of pain: there was no other way. I would either be hurt or hurt in my turn: being human I could not remain neutral. I met the girl with extreme reluctance; and wondered at her motives for wishing to confront me with her story.

Her appearance did nothing to allay my fears; in fact, it increased what I already felt would be a momentous and disturbing meeting. I remember her now as looking very child-like: she had the sort of paedophilic look of a small elf—which some men find appealing. She was tense and anxious, as though at some point she had taken the decision to hold back. I did not like her much. I find that sort of woman manipulative; full of little betrayals, because of all the insecurity of her knowing that she did not rank among the women. Fear was written all over her face.

She looked as if she were on the run from something. And I knew, because I had seen such cases before, that she was haunted. During our opening small talk her utterances came out in jagged phrases, exclamations, sentences begun then abandoned, then taken up with a different subject: she made so many promising beginnings yet never knew quite how to complete them. But in relation to one thing she was utterly articulate: the story she told.

This, then, was how she began:

"When I was thirteen I was invited to spend the long summer vacation at the home of a friend who lived in Dublin. Sheelagh Burke was at school with me, we both attended the Dominican Convent in Portstewart. I was a day-girl; my father owned a newspaper shop in the Diamond in Portstewart. Sheelagh was a boarder; her parents lived in Dublin, where her father had something to do with property investment. I was never very clear. The thing about the upper middle classes even in Ireland is that the source of their income is never very precisely located; it is only a petty bourgeois mentality like mine which would seek to pin people to their incomes."

The girl had a disconcerting habit of standing back and analysing her statements—placing them in a social context thereby dismissing her own assumptions. Her tutor said she was a natural historian, if only she had the confidence to follow it through. I understood too that there had been some disturbance in her studies of a few years, but was not clear about the nature of this, and had not asked. These thoughts were going through my mind as she continued.

"My parents were delighted at the invitation: this was precisely why they had wanted me to go to grammar school—to make friends like Sheelagh Burke. The Burke house at Sandycove was not far from here, and it was remarkable. It was at the far end of that long stretch of coast road which runs away from Trinity corner in the direction of the Dun Laoghaire ferry terminal, beyond the Martello Tower and still further. I remember arriving there so well. The house formed part of a terrace set back from the main road. There was a small green in front and a gravel path or drive separated the green from the four double-fronted Georgian houses which stood there; the house belonging to the Burkes was the last of the four—that is, the one furthest from Dublin city. Like the other houses it was three storeys high and had a basement, with a separate entrance by the railings outside the front door. The basement was something new in the way of houses to me. In a seaside town like Portstewart there is only the unrelenting parade of low-lying bungalows in wide bare salt-stripped gardens, occasionally relieved by some modern two-storey houses, a row or two of Victorian terraces and of course the Convent itself, a castle of Gothic proportions perched on the cliff face. I had never been in a house with a basement before, and absolutely nothing of the neighbourhood I grew up in equalled the elegance of this fine wide-roomed house, with its brass handles and porticoes, wooden stairways and cornices. A further treat was still to come with that house—the waves of the Irish Sea broke upon the back wall. The garden literally ran away to the sea. From the music-room windows we had uninterrupted views of the sea and the day marked out for us by the comings and goings of the Holyhead ferry.

I was given a room at the top of the house on the same floor as Sheelagh and Peggy—who lived in—and the view from my window was of Howth Head. I even remember the colour of the room: it was a strong bold rose colour and the walls were full of prints of flowers and birds. The curtains matched the cover on the bed. I recorded every detail of this house, committed it to memory like I did my Latin grammar. I never questioned that this too was part of my general education. After a time it became clear to me why I had been asked to spend the summer with Sheelagh; she was lonely, there wasn't anyone else around. Her parents were remarkable by their absence. Her father, whom we saw fleetingly, flew in and out of Dublin airport with such regularity it made my head spin. Places like Zurich, Munich and New York crept in the conversation by way of explaining these disappearances. I think I met her mother as she was passing through the music room one day on her way to lunch. And even though she lived in the house and was not flying in and out of the country, we saw even less of her. I recall that she said something like: 'Hello, you're Sheelagh's little friend aren't you. How nice of you to come.' The only other inhabitants of the house appeared to be a brother who was a student at UCD, reading Medicine or some suitably middle-class professional subject. Peggy, whom I have already mentioned, was a sort of housekeeper cum Nanny; her role was never very clearly defined. And as Peggy was slow on her feet and found the stairs too much from time to time, there was a young girl living in also to help. She lived in the basement and was called Moraig. I said that Sheelagh's brother was an inhabitant, that was not strictly true; he had a flat somewhere in the city, and only came home at weekends to eat Peggy's Sunday lunch.

You can imagine from this that we spent a good deal of time on our own, Sheelagh and I. We played tennis, or went swimming off the rocks at the bottom of the garden; occasionally we took long bus rides into the city and ended up having tea and cakes at Bewleys. I had never had tea in a café before, and certainly not without an adult present. It seemed to me, because of the absence of adults in our lives that summer, that we had in fact grown up; the world was unmoved by our innocence. When we ordered tea in Bewleys it appeared. No one said, as they might have done in a tea shop at home, 'What are you two children up to?' They took us seriously in Dublin. I felt I had entered a newly sophisticated world. In a few short weeks

17

of being at that house, my confidence grew. I discovered that beds left unmade were magically made up. Clothes, even socks, could be hurled around the room with no fear of losing them; they would reappear fresh and clean a few days later. The best china and glass was used without restraint; and, even if broken, was always replaced or renewed without fuss. It put all my mother's restraints and little fussy ways in perspective: 'If you don't pick that up you will lose it; if you don't tidy that away it won't last; we can't use the best china we might break it.' For the first time I felt I had an answer to her. What did it matter when life could be lived like this? I knew then that something was ruined for me. I have dwelt rather long on this beginning because I wanted to remember what it was like up to the point when everything changed, and not try to suppress any of the details. Perhaps, though, I have romanticized it a little, but I don't think so. The important thing is this is how it impressed me.

The music room, as it was called, was a long rectangle running from front to back of the house on the ground floor. It was a very grand room with a wide marble fireplace, two squashy sofas and a couple of battered armchairs; it had a sanded pine floor and a large indestructible and rather tatty rug—which Sheelagh said was Indian. This was considered the children's room. It had been abandoned to the Burke children several years before; the smarter apartments and drawing room, which was out of bounds to us, were on the floor above. I never knew why it earned the name the music room, except perhaps it might have referred to the volume of noise emanating from it; because the only concession to a musical instrument that I could see was an upright piano which nobody appeared to play or knew how to, standing against the same wall as the fireplace. On the opposite wall to the piano and the fireplace ran row upon row of silent books, and I believe there was a record player somewhere. But I can't quite remember where it was situated. Long small-paned windows filled the short walls at either end of the room so that the light ran right through. From the Sandycove road to the Irish Sea the view was uninterrupted.

In the evenings when the wind coming off the sea rattled the windows, it was often quite noisy and indeed airy in the music room, even after the curtains were drawn. And it was on one such occasion while sitting in front of the fire with the wind fanning the flames, when Moraig had retreated to her basement, and Peggy was in bed with a cold, that we conceived of the idea of whiling away the evening by telling ghost stories. That is, I would. Sheelagh never told stories. In fact, she could never remember the important details, and she would often have to turn to me and say: 'What comes next? I forget.'

I began with a favourite of both of us. I was not very original. I often told the same story twice, but usually with embellishments or twists. And Sheelagh was such a good listener and such an awful rememberer that every time she heard the story she said it sounded different. This encouraged me tremendously. I began with a story of Le Fanu's about the expected visitors who never arrive: at one point in the evening the family who are waiting for the visitors hear the sound of carriage wheels roll on the gravel, they all rush outside and find no one. What I had not allowed for when I was telling this favourite tale of ours, was the fact that right outside the music room was a gravel drive. And, at precisely the part in the story when I started to explain that at the time the family heard the wheels of the carriage on the gravel, the expected visitor had died, at precisely that moment a car drew up very slowly on the gravel drive outside the music-room window. Sheelagh took one leap off the carpet where we were sitting in front of the fire and fled out of the room, saying that she didn't want to hear any more. I was left in the music room, still sitting in front of the fire, amazed at her alacrity. Normally, I would have been laughing myself sick at my ability to scare her, as I had often done in the past, but the trouble was this time I had scared myself. The massive coincidence necessary to tell an effective ghost story had just

19

occurred. At precisely the time when I was explaining the significance of ghostly wheels on gravel as a portent of death—a car drew up. In all my years of telling ghost stories at school, and arranging for bells to ring or doors to open at crucial moments, I had never stage-managed anything so effective as that car drawing up when it did.

I found myself sitting in the dark of the room with only the light from the fire throwing grotesque shadows on to the walls and the groans of the wind whistling around me as company. I knew then that I could not bring myself to move through the darkness towards the door or beyond into the dark hall and then up three flights of stairs past all those closed doorways and little landings to my bed. I was riveted. So I stayed sitting still with my back to the fire, watching the silent occupants of the darkness, until I calmed down. Once or twice I imagined I saw the handle of the door turning, so I tried to think of something pleasant. But when I looked away to the window all the elements of stories I had told in broad daylight on the beach, or in the gym or the second-form common room, began to reassemble around me. And I wished I hadn't had such a fertile imagination. Then, just when I managed to convince myself of my silliness and was beginning to work out how I could make another story out of this incident, something happened which arrested me so completely that I thought my heart would stop. From behind me in the fire I heard a little cry; not a groan, like the wind made, of that I am absolutely clear. It began like a short gasp and became a rising crescendo of 'hah' sounds; each one was following the one before, and getting louder each time. I experienced a moment of such pure terror that I felt my heart would burst with the strain as I waited for the gasps to reach their topmost note. Suddenly, just when the sounds had come to a peak, I felt myself propelled from the room and ran screaming upstairs. I take no responsibility for that action; a voice simply broke from my throat which corresponded to screams.

In this state, I ran up three flights and straight into the arms of the warm, white-clad and still smelling of sleep Peggy. She had been under sedation all day because of her cold when the screams brought her to the banisters. Sheelagh was standing behind her, clutching Peggy's nightgown and howling like a lost dog. Peggy was furious rather than consoling I seem to remember. She smacked both of us to make me stop screeching and Sheelagh stop howling, and then asked us what we thought we were up to. 'Bringing the house down like that' was how she put it. Characteristically Sheelagh blamed me for scaring her by telling the story; I blamed her for leaving me downstairs. Peggy resorted to her usual threats of 'Right Madam. You go straight back to Portstewart in the morning. Do ye hear?' And for the first time in the six weeks I had been there I wished she meant it. I had had enough of the freedom of the place; inside, a small voice that I thought I had grown out of was saying: 'Oh Mammy, I want to go home.' Eventually, she got us both back to bed. Calmed, and much scolded, and therefore reassured, I went to sleep.

I am always afraid to go to sleep. I have been ever since that time, and still have lingering doubts about it. It has something to do with going to sleep with one reality and waking up with another. It was like this on that particular morning. It was late when I woke; the morning boat to Holyhead leaving Dun Laoghaire was already filling the space in the horizon between the shore and Howth Head at the half-way point. I did not wake up myself as I normally do, but was wakened instead by the arrival of Peggy carrying breakfast. She told me to eat up and get dressed and come downstairs when I was ready. There were two men who wished to talk to me. Sheelagh, she explained, was already awake and I could see her after I spoke to the men. She busied herself picking up my clothes and laying things out while I ate breakfast. What surprised me was that she stayed until I had finished and then supervised my washing. I had reached the stage where I was bashful about dressing and wished she would go. But she didn't. When I was ready we went downstairs. I was

absolutely convinced now that something momentous had
occurred. 'How come Moraig didn't bring breakfast this
morning?' I asked, as I reached the foot of the stairs with the
tray. Looking back, I am amazed at the ease with which I had
become accustomed to being waited upon. Peggy did not
answer but said: 'Come and meet the gentlemen who would like
to talk to you.' We went into the music room and I have to admit
to experiencing a momentary shudder as we passed through the
door.

My suspicions were further confirmed at finding Sheelagh's
father there, along with two men. The room looked different in
the morning light; below, the boat was still slipping past Howth
and out to the open sea. On the other side of me I caught sight of
a number of cars parked on the green verge; there were some
people moving up and down the basement steps. One of the men
in the room moved between me and this view from the window.
He shook hands and called himself Mr Maguire. He then
introduced the other stranger, his friend Mr O'Rourke. I can't
recall much of what they looked like except that they were both
tall and Mr Maguire was heavier than Mr O'Rourke. But I
guessed that they were policemen.

'We want you tell us now,' said Maguire, 'what it was that
made you scream out last night.'

I couldn't believe it; I turned to Peggy in alarm. Had she
called the police because I had screamed? Before I could reply,
Sheelagh's father uttered the first words he had ever spoken to
me.

'Now don't worry, just tell Mr Maguire what happened. No
one is going to hurt you.'

Peggy squeezed my arm to encourage me I expect, but
immediately I decided that this was precisely what they would
do—hurt me—and burst into loud sobs. When I stopped
crying, they persisted with the questions and so I explained how
the ghost story had frightened us. I explained about the wheels
on the gravel drive; how Sheelagh had fled from the room

leaving me; how I sat on until I thought I heard sounds coming from the fire behind me.

'Voices from the flame?' Mr O'Rourke said, looking meaningfully. 'You heard a voice talking to you from out of the fire?'

'Now that's enough Jack!' Maguire said.

'Well not exactly a voice talking, more calling out,' I explained. I am quite convinced that O'Rourke felt himself in the presence of a mystic who was in touch with speaking flames. But the other policeman wasn't so sure about the presence of the Holy Ghost in the proceedings, he kept bringing me back to what I actually did hear.

'Can you repeat the sounds you thought you heard?' he asked.

'I'm not sure,' I said, 'but I'll try.'

I began to call in the way I thought I had heard the voice call out the evening before. To make the sound I had to take short gasps, and eventually when I was quite breathless I stopped.

'Why did you stop?' Maguire asked.

'Because I didn't hear the rest,' I explained.

'Why?'

'Because I was screaming so loudly at the time.'

And that was all. The interview was over and so was the holiday. Sheelagh and her father drove me to the station later and I did return to Portstewart on that day after all. I would have been glad enough about it except that I felt I was going home in some disgrace, and I was not exactly sure why. Sheelagh spoke very little to me, she seemed very downcast, and told me that she was being sent to an aunt in the West of Ireland for the rest of the summer. 'I hate it there. I'll go mad with boredom,' she said. The last time I saw her she was waving goodbye from the platform at Connelly Station. She did not return to school in September, and she did not write to me as she promised. My parents never questioned my early return as I was sure they would. I gave up telling stories after that."

"But what happened?" I asked. I found myself growing impatient. "And what has all this to do with dreams?"

"You're rushing me," she said. "And I have to unfold it slowly. They never told me and I didn't ask because somewhere deep down I already knew that it was something profoundly disturbing. Then, one day, when seven years had passed, the truth surfaced to confront me, and this is what happened. I went to Queen's as a first-year history student in '68; the first year of the disturbances in the city. But I wasn't really interested in politics and knew little about what was happening, except that there were mass meetings in the union, the McMordie Hall and in the streets. It was the beginning of the civil rights movement, when educated Catholics had awakened to political conscious-ness. Coming from Portstewart I never had any sense of the discrimination that Catholics in the city seemed to feel. It never occurred to me that there were official and unofficial histories. Or that Protestants could go through school never having heard of Parnell or the Land League. I always thought that history was simply a matter of scholarship. In the seminars during my first year at university the students were fighting and hacking and forging out of the whole mass of historical detail a theory which made it right for them to march through the streets of Belfast to demand equal rights for Catholics. It was the most exciting year of my life; inevitably I fell in love.

He was a counterpoint to everything my father with his little shop and cautious peace-keeping ways stood for. He was outspoken and clever and courageous; he didn't care who he offended, and he held back for nothing and no one. Until that time I had spent my whole life living on the edge of the kind of respectability that people who run a corner shop find necessary in order to secure a trade and therefore their livelihood. I had heard my father humour the diverse opinions of so many of the customers that I grew to believe opinions were something one expressed but did not necessarily believe in, or indeed act upon. As we ran a newsagent's it became the venue for discussion of

24

current events, particularly on a Sunday morning, when the locals would stroll in to collect the 'sundies' and debate the week's news at leisure.

'It's about time O'Neill got the finger out over this free-trade business. Why should Lemass do all the running?'

'Ah, now, Mr O'Neill's a good man,' I can hear my father interrupt. 'He sends his girl to the convent. Did you know that?'

'No, it's not the same O'Neill. You're thinking of the brother.'

'It's not a brother; he's the man's uncle.'

'That's just the trouble, the government's full of O'Neills; it's very confusing.'

My father always had a good word to say about everyone. If any politician was criticized he was quick to find some redeeming feature. With the result that I too became something of an apologist when it came to historical circumstances. That is, until I found myself walking en route from the university to the City Hall beside a provoking and thoroughly objectionable undergraduate: John Mulhern. I remember going home for the weekend following some of the first civil rights marches Belfast had witnessed, and finding my father fuming over the early dispatches of the Sunday papers.

'Fools and trouble-makers that's all they are! We have a fine, peaceful little country here. What do they have to go making trouble for?'

I kept my involvement a secret and refused to be drawn into any of the discussions in the shop which ranged during the eleven o'clock Mass. It was a feature of most Sunday mornings that the women went to Mass while the men stayed in the papershop. Then I heard my father say, 'I can't afford a political viewpoint!' as someone tried to draw him out. 'That is a political viewpoint—pure petty bourgeoisie self-interest' was my unexpected reply. It came straight out of the mouth of John Mulhern. I knew I should not have said it (a) because I couldn't justify it, and (b) because I had as good as betrayed my father by taking sides against him in the shop. There was a deafening silence, so much so that you could actually hear the waves crashing along the wall of the promenade some distance down the hill.

'That's the stuff! You young ones with your education will tell them boys at Stormont where to get off!' said the man who had provoked the row in the first place. My father, whose anger was all in his face until that point, burst out, 'If that's all the good a university education has done for you, I rue the day you ever went to that place.'

The conversation was over. I fled into the back of the shop and he followed me. 'Your mother and I broke our backs scraping and saving to give you a chance. If this is how you repay us you can take yourself out of here back to your friends in Belfast with their clever remarks and smart ways; but don't ever come here again, shaming me in front of my friends.'

We never talked about anything important after that; I withdrew and so did they. I was thrown almost completely on to my friends in the city until I ceased to come home at all. My parents had ceased to expect me to. Occasionally I suppose they would read about this march or that and would guess I was there.

This is peripheral I know, but I am coming to the point. I said that the truth about that summer all those years before reappeared at a particular moment. I have given you all this detail because I am a historian and a materialist and somewhere in all these factors an answer may emerge as to why at this particular period in my life the truth, or a perception, should become clear to me.

It was the sixth of January when we returned to Belfast from Derry after the civil rights march which had taken four days to reach Derry had been attacked at Burntollet Bridge. I remember we, John and I, and two other students who lived in his house, were all feeling very fragile, very tired, and yet strangely elated. Something had been brought to the surface in the façade of political life—the cracks were throwing all sorts of horrors out into the sunlight. I had never slept with John before until that night.

We had begun to make love and I was lying back in the dark looking at him. I closed my eyes and suddenly I found myself crying out in a way which was strangely familiar: I uttered or heard myself utter a series of small gasps until at the point when the note rose to its highest point I opened my eyes. Then I screamed and screamed and screamed. I imagined that John would strangle me and screamed out in terror. After that the room was full of lights and voices. As soon as the lights came on of course I was no longer afraid of him. The other students in the house thought I ought to have a sedative so a doctor was called. He tried to get me to take a sleeping pill, but I only wanted to rid myself of what I knew. 'She was murdered. Moraig was murdered. He strangled her.' I was rambling on incoherently, as it must have appeared to the onlookers, trying to piece together parts of the story of seven years before. I felt bombarded by signs and images and the meaning of events. They persisted in making me take the sleeping pill and so I gave in. Afterwards I resented having done so, because when I did reawaken I knew that I had passed from that state for ever, and would never arrive at a perception so intensely felt again. With the morning and the new awareness my parents came, and with them a chill. As though they had brought with them the bleak wind which blows in off the Atlantic along the prom and leaves small deposits of sea-salt in the corners of their mouths. I felt the ice kisses on my damp cheek and tasted the bitterness of those salt-years. Before them lay the wreck of a daughter in whom they have invested everything.

The last communication I had with my parents prior to that day was a letter from my mother on the first of January wishing me well for the New Year and informing me of the death of Sheelagh Burke. She had driven off a cliff at Westpoint—near her aunt's house in Galway a few days before. There is a faint irony in that; her banishment was from Dublin to Westpoint seven years before. It was as though everything had come full circle; some strange mystery had unravelled—wound down. I seem to remember that the tone of my mother's letter was half-reproachful as though in Sheelagh's death was some responsibility of mine. I put the letter in my bag and took it with me on the march; but I lost it somewhere on the road to Derry. I explain this detail again because it may also have been a factor prompting the truth of that evening when Moraig was murdered to the surface of my mind. You see, I too had come to feel that the whole event was the result of some strange invocation of mine. I had called up, or dreamed up, the death just as surely as if I had murdered Moraig."

"But you didn't dream it; you say it happened!" I said, reminding her.

"I haven't told you the rest of the story."

"So far you haven't told me anything original: this is either Sleeping Beauty or Alice in Wonderland!" I said irritably. "But please go on."

"Haven't you realized yet that at precisely the moment in my story when I was explaining the significance of wheels on the gravel drive as a sign of death, the car carrying the murderer drew up? I created the event. What is more I later heard a woman making love up to the point of strangulation when I began screaming for her. It was no mystical experience: I heard her cries coming up through the chimney passage. Apparently her bed was right next to the boxed-in fireplace in the basement. When I sat with my back to the fireplace I heard everything. Seven years later when I made love for the first time I re-experienced the earlier memory and found the truth."

"The truth?"

"Yes. When I was making love and I opened my eyes one split second before I screamed out, I saw something. The face I was

28

looking at was not the face of my lover."

"Whose face did you see?"

"I saw Sheelagh's brother. I saw John Burke's face."

We regarded each other openly for the first time, in the way two human beings do when the mask has slipped—stripped away by either love or fear—and familiar traces of another remembering show through.

"At what point in the story did you recognize me?" she asked.

"Very early on; but I wanted to hear you out. At one point you almost had me believing you were someone else. I found myself thinking that I was listening to another coincidental story. You changed the names and the house location; that was imaginative. But you rather over-dramatized my sister's death. She did not drive off the cliff at Westpoint. She died of a heroin overdose in a basement flat in Islington. She had become a drop-out a few years before and we lost touch with her. So you see reality is more ignominious. Still she would have liked your version better—it romanticized her. But then I seem to remember you have a panache for that. Why did you come here with this memory? I find it all very painful."

"Why did I come?"

She had no sympathy for my pain; I had not stopped her but made her angry instead.

"You can ask me that? I have spent three years of my life in a hospital. Did you know?"

I shook my head.

"I can't sleep with the light out; I can't lie in the dark in case I see your face. For three years I took their drugs and their treatments but I kept my secret because I knew that the one thing which would cure me was that one day I would be able to confront you with the truth."

"The truth? What is the truth?"

"You killed Moraig."

"Your hallucination of one face on to another isn't proof of a person being a murderer."

"Not proof—truth!" she said emphatically. "The imagination presents or dramatizes as well as intuiting a reality which is nearer the truth than any perception we arrive at through understanding, that is what I believe. And that is what I came here to find out. If I haven't awoken to reality after all this time, then I have awoken to madness. If I'm not through to truth then I'm through to madness. I believe you murdered Moraig because I saw your face."

"Have you told anyone else?"

"No one—not until now," she said. "I need an admission from you—not a denial. I am either sane or mad."

"It's metaphysics. Sanity or insanity," I said.

"It's not metaphysics. It's the difference between truth and lies."

"Let me give you a better explanation of what happened— one you can live with. The car drawing up was a coincidence; it may or may not have had something to do with the murderer's arrival. But two half-hysterical little girls managed to convince themselves that they heard it and so it must be like that. A servant girl, Moraig, was murdered by her lover; and you heard her cries as you said, through the chimney passage. Now there is another factor which you haven't mentioned. One of those little girls had a massive crush on her friend's brother. She also knew that he was friendly with Moraig. She knew because she sometimes watched him; and perhaps she saw them exchanging glances. Isn't it possible that you saw his face when your lover—also called John—was making love to you for the first time because that was the face you wanted to see? You fused the murder of Moraig and the desire to see me into one single incident. And you went to great lengths to say how much you loved this other John—I found it a total diversion, an unconvincing obsession with that part of the story. Was it in case I guessed that you chose him for the resemblance between the names? John's name and mine are the same in reality and in the story. Why?"

30

"Because I wanted you to remember," she said. "I wanted to see your fear, as you have seen mine. Nothing you have said convinces me that you did not kill Moraig."

"Don't persist with this," I warned her. "I've offered you a way out. You have a strong healthy young mind now—don't pursue this fantasy path any further."

"That is exactly why I came to see you. To find my way back to a path I once knew. I don't want an explanation or a denial but I need an admission of your guilt before I can break out of this . . ." She paused as though she knew the word but could not use it; it came out eventually ". . . nightmare!"

At that point she began to cry.

I watched her very closely and realized for the first time that she was wrong; she did not need an admission; she was already free. In the telling of her story she had changed. She had lost the haunted look: she had confessed. After a while when she was quieter, I asked: "What became of John Mulhern—your lover? You didn't say."

"After that night it wasn't the same between us. He was afraid of me, and I think I was of him. I was taken home for a while to Portstewart and nursed by my mother. A short time after that I was admitted to a sanatorium, as I have already told you. I came to Dublin only this year, to resume my studies. They thought I was better out of the North. He became something in the paramilitary, and is very well known. I heard that he married someone recently, but I don't recall the details."

"He didn't wait for you to heal?"

"No. He didn't wait."

It was that time of day when the Holyhead ferry has passed the tip of Howth on its journey out to open sea; the sun shone on the rocks at Sandycove, and a woman, young, but a woman none the less—faint lines around the mouth marked her out—standing by a window, traced its slow passage forth. There

31

would be many comings and goings to and from the shore, and many more passages to make as time went by; but at that moment, all her attention was with this one.

I looked away from the window; and found myself alone in the room.

The Journey to Somewhere Else

The snowroad to the Alps runs south-east from Lyons to Chambéry whereafter, leaving the autoroute behind, it takes up with a steep mountain road north to Mégève on the western slopes of Mont Blanc.

The resort café, several miles above the village, was full of seventeen-year-old French millionaires—or so it seemed to us—and large Italian families: the women wore fur hats with their ski-suits and too many rings for comfort; their men had paunches and smoked cigars at lunch; and the twelve-year-old Italian girls confirmed for all time that fourteen was the only age to marry and Capulet's daughter might never have been such a catch had she lived long enough to look like her mother. There were probably some large French families as well, but they were less inclined to sit together as a group. The resort on the borders with Switzerland and Italy was fairly cosmopolitan; confirming too that the rich, like their money, are not different but indifferent to frontiers. Whatever nation they came from, they had nannies for their children, who cut up the food at different tables and did not ski. On Christmas Day opposite me a black woman peeled a small orange and fed it to a fat white child, piece by piece. The smell did it: Satsumas!

Christmas Day in '59; they ran the buses in Belfast; the pungent smell of orange brought it back. My brother, the satsumas in green and red silver paper on the piano in the parlour, the fire dying in the grate and the adults asleep in their rooms. And that year, in '59 when I was eight, it had begun to snow. The grate-iron to rest the kettle on squeaked as I pushed it towards the coals with my foot.

"You'll burn your slipper soles," Michael John said.

"I'm bored."

"We could go out."

"How?"

"The bus passes to the City Hall every fifteen minutes."

"They'll not allow us. I've no money and—"

"Ah go on, Amee. I dare you," he said. "Run out, catch the next bus to the City Hall and come back up on it without paying."

"But the conductor will put me off!"

"That's the dare. See how far you can get. The person who gets furthest wins!"

My brother was small and fair and mischievous; there was ten months' difference in our ages.

"All right then, I'll go."

Joe is dark and tall and mostly silent; there is ten years between us.

"Would you like me to get one for you?" Joe said, putting the lunch tray on the table in front of me. "Amee, would you like one?"

"What?"

"The oranges you keep staring at," he said, handing me a glass of cold red wine.

"I'm sorry. No. I don't really like them very much."

"You're shivering."

"The wine's so cold."

"Grumble. Grumble."

"I'm sorry."

With the life in the room the windows in the café clouded over.

"It would help if you stopped breathing," he joked, as the window next to us misted.

34

The Journey to Somewhere Else

It was a doomed journey from the start. Like all our holidays together, it was full of incidents, mishaps and narrow escapes. Once, in Crete, I nearly drowned. I fell off his mother's boyfriend's boat and swallowed too much water. I remember coming up for air and watching him staring at me from the deck; he had been a lifesaver on a beach one summer, but I swam to those rocks myself. Four years ago in Switzerland, where he was working at the time, I fell on a glacier mountain, the Jungfrau, and slid headlong towards the edge with my skis behind me. I screamed for several minutes before I realized that if I continued to panic I would probably break my neck. I stopped screaming and thought about saving myself. At which point everything slowed down and I turned my body round on the snow, put my skis between me and the icy ridge and came to a halt. When I had enough energy I climbed back up. I suppose what happened this time was inevitable. About an hour after we crossed the Channel he crashed the car in Béthune. He drove at speed into the back of the one in front. I saw the crash coming and held my breath. On the passenger side we ended up minus a headlamp and with a very crumpled wing.

"Why didn't you shout if you saw it coming?" he objected later.

"It seemed a waste of energy," I said. "I couldn't have prevented it happening."

We exchanged it for a French car at Arrais and after I travelled apprehensively towards the Alps.

"Why don't we ski separately?" I suggested, after the first week. "I'd like some ski lessons. Anyway, you're a far more advanced skier. I only hold you back."

On the second day of that week I came back from ski class at four thirty and waited for him in the café by the main telecabin. There were so few people inside now the glass was almost clear. A family group sat at one table and the ski instructors at the bar drank cognac. I waited for half an hour before I noticed the time.

It was snowing heavily outside then as well, and even getting dark. The snow was turning blue in the light. I closed the heavy front door behind me lightly till the snib caught and ran across the road to wait at the stop. I could see him watching at the lace curtains in the sitting room. The Christmas-tree lights were on in the room, the curtain shifted. Soundlessly, the bus arrived. I got on, and just as quietly it moved off. The conductor was not on the platform, nor was he on the lower deck, so I went to the front and crouched low on the seat and hoped he wouldn't notice me when he did appear. There was no one else aboard but two old ladies in hats with shopping baskets and empty Lucozade bottles. Noisily, the conductor came downstairs. He stood on the platform clinking small change; I could see his reflection in the glass window of the driver's seat. If I was lucky he would not bother me, I was too far away from the platform. Suddenly, he started to walk up the bus. I looked steadfastly out of the window. He rapped the glass pane to the driver and said something. The driver nodded. He spoke again. I was in such terror of a confrontation that I didn't hear anything he said. For a moment he glanced in my direction, and he remained where he stood. We were nearing the cinemas at the end of the road. At this point I decided not to go all the way round the route to the City Hall. I got up quickly and walked down the bus away from him and stood uneasily on the platorm. At the traffic lights before the proper stop, he moved along the bus towards me, my nerve failed and I leaped off.

"Hey!" he called out. "You can't get off here."

It was snowing more heavily. Wet snow. My feet were cold. I looked down and saw that I was still wearing my slippers; red felt slippers with a pink fur trim. How strange I must have looked in a duffel coat and slippers in the snow. The clock of the Presbyterian Assembly Buildings read five forty-five. It chimed on the quarter-hour, and behind me the lights of a closed-up

confectioner's illuminated a man I had not noticed
before. 'You'll get your nice slippers wet," he said.

"I'll dry them when I get home," I said.

"You'll get chilblains that way."

"No I won't."

I looked doubtfully at my slippers; the red at the toes was
darker than the rest and my feet felt very uncomfortable.

"Have you far to walk when you get off the bus?" he asked.

"No. I live just up the road. The bus passes my house," I
said.

"You'd better stand in here. It's drier," he said.

I didn't answer. At that moment a young woman came round
the corner into view and began walking towards us from the
town centre. She walked with difficulty through the snow in
high shoes. Under her coat a black dress and white apron
showed as she moved. The woman looked at me and then at the
man and stopped. She drew a packet of cigarettes from her
apron pocket and lit one. At first she waited at the stop with me,
and then, shivering, moved back into the protective shelter of
the shop front by the man's side.

"That wind 'ud go clean through you so it would," she said.

"Aye. It comes in off the Lough and goes straight up the
Black Mountain," he said, looking away up the road. The
woman and I followed his gaze.

Beyond us, a block or two away, was the dolls' hospital, we
had been there a few weeks before with my mother.

"Leave the aeroplanes alone, Michael John!" she scolded.
"Just wait and see what Santa brings you."

I loved that shop with all its dolls, repaired, redressed. My
own doll had started out from there as a crinoline lady in white
net with hoops and red velvet bows. That year, when we left it at
the shop minus a leg it had been returned to me as a Spanish
dancer in a petticoat of multicoloured layers. We only ever
visited the town with my mother; during the day when it was
busy and friendly, when the matinées at the cinema were going

37

in and the traffic moved round the centre, the cinema confectioner's shop in front of which I stood was always open and sold rainbow drops and white chocolate mice—the latter turned up in my stocking—so were there too, I noticed for the first time, satsumas in that window.

The snow, and the quiet and the darkness had transformed the town. In the blue-grey light the charm of the life went out of it, it seemed unfamiliar, dead. I wanted to go home to the fire in the parlour; I began to shiver convulsively, and then the bus came.

"Ardoyne." The woman looked out. "That's my bus."

I was so grateful I forgot about the dare.

"No good to you?" she said to the man.

He shook his head and pulled up the collar of his coat.

"Merry Christmas," she called out as we got on.

I was sitting brazenly at the seat next to the platform when the conductor turned to me for the fare.

"I forgot my purse," I said. "But this bus passes my house, my Mammy'll pay it when I get home."

"Oh your Mammy'll pay it when you get home!" he mimicked. "Did you hear that now!"

The young woman, who had gone a little further up the bus, turned round. We had only moved a couple of streets beyond the stop, the toyshop was behind me. A wire cage encased its shop front.

"Please don't put me off now," I said, beginning to cry.

"I'll pay her fare," the young woman said.

"Does you Mammy know you're out at all?" he asked and, getting no answer moved along to the woman. "Where are you going to anyway?" he called back.

"The stop before the hospital stop," I said weakly.

"The Royal," he said to the woman. The ticket machine rolled once.

"And Ardoyne. The terminus," she said.

The ticket machine rolled once more and they grumbled

between them about having to work on Christmas Day.

"I'll be late getting my dinner tonight. Our ones'll all have finished when I get in."

"Aye sure I know. I'm not off till eight," he said. "It's hardly been worth it. The one day in the year." He snapped the tickets off the roll and gave her change. "And no overtime."

Someone, a man, clambered downstairs to the platform. He had a metal tin under his arm. The conductor pulled the bell.

"No overtime? You're kiddin'," she said.

"That's the Corporation for you," he said.

Before the hospital stop he pulled the bell again. I stepped down to the platform. I could see the Christmas-tree lights in the bay window of the parlour. I jumped off and ran towards the house, and wished that I hadn't been too ashamed to thank her. But her head was down and she wasn't looking after me.

Michael John opened the door: "You did it?" he said, half in awe. "I saw you get off the bus. You did it!"

"Yes," I gasped. My heart was pounding and my feet hurt.

"All the way to the City Hall?"

"Of course."

He followed me into the parlour.

"But look at your slippers, Amee, they're ruined. You went out in your slippers. They'll know."

"Not if I dry them. No one will ever know."

I put my slippers on the fender and stood looking at the red dye on the toes of my white tights. I pulled off the stockings as well and saw that even my toes were stained.

"Look at that, Michael John! My toes are dyed!" I said. "Michael John?"

The front door closed so quietly it was hardly audible.

"Michael John! Don't go!"

From the sitting-room window I could see him crossing the road.

"Oh I only pretended," I breathed. "I didn't."

But he was too far away. And then the bus came.

I waited at that window until my breathing clouded the glass. I rubbed it away with my fist. Every now and then I checked the slippers drying at the fender. Gradually the dark red faded, the toes curled up and only a thin white line remained. I went back to the window and listened for the bus returning. Several buses did come by, but Michael John did not. I got under the velvet drapes and the lace and stood watching at the glass where the cold is trapped and waited. I would tell him the truth when he came back. The overhead lights of the sitting room blazed on and my mother's voice called:

"Ameldia! What are you doing there?"

She looked crossly round the room.

"You've even let the fire go out! Where is Michael John?"

"Excusez-moi? Madame Fitzgerald?" the waitress in the café asked.

My ski pass lay on the table, she glanced at it briefly; the photograph and the name reassured her.

"Telephone!" she said, indicating that I should follow.

The ski instructors at the bar turned their heads to watch as I passed by to the phone. They were the only group left in the café. I expected to hear Joe's voice, instead a woman at the other end of the line spoke rapid French.

"Please. Could you speak English?" I asked.

She repeated her message.

"Your friend is here at the clinic in the village. We have X-rayed him. He will now return to your hotel. Can you please make your own way back."

"Yes. But what is wrong?"

"I'm sorry?"

"What is wrong with him?"

"An accident. Not serious."

"Thank you," I said, and hurried away from the phone.

Outside it was dark and still snowing. I knew two routes back to the village: there was the mountain route we had skied down on after class a few days before, half an hour earlier by the light; and there was the route by road which we had driven up on in the morning. I could also take the bus. It was five twenty. The lifts and telecabins closed nearly an hour before. The bus which met the end of ski class had long gone; so too had the skiers to the town. The only people left seemed to be resort staff and instructors, most of whom lived on the mountain. It took five minutes to ski down to the village on the mountain, and forty-five minutes to go by road—if a bus came. Without further hesitation I made the decision to take the shortest route back. It was too dark to ski, so I put my skis on my shoulder and started out to walk along the ski-track down the mountain.

I followed the path confidently at first, encouraged by the sight of three young men who were walking fairly swiftly ahead. Half-way down the hill through a farm, which even in deep snow smelt of farming, I passed a woman, going in the opposite direction, who looked at me briefly and said:

"Bonsoir, madame."

The surprise in her voice and the weight of the skis on my shoulder arrested me momentarily so I stopped: "Bonsoir."

I shifted the skis to my other shoulder and in so doing realized that I had lost sight of the walkers ahead. I walked on to a turning point by a chalet and found there that the path forked two ways. There was no one ahead anymore, and looking back uphill I found that the woman had disappeared. The lights of the village twinkled before me, directly below the treeline, luring me down the slope. The other path stretched more gradually down around the mountain. In the light it had been so easy. I stood for a moment staring at the mute grey wetness. Were there really two tracks? The longer I stood in the dark looking, the more confusing it became. If I don't move now it will be too late. I moved. I set off again rapidly downhill, but the weight of the skis on my shoulder and the slippery gradient propelled me onwards at a hair-raising speed towards the treeline. The hard plastic boots made it impossible to grip the

41

snow. I slipped badly and then stopped suddenly against the slope. My legs shook. I was breathless. If I moved another inch I would probably break a leg. Lost. I'm lost as well. If I could only be sure that this was the right way. Perhaps the wider more gradual path is the one. I set off to climb back to the fork again. A light in the chalet further up the slope reassured me. I could always ask there.

Breathless, I regained the beginning of the two paths. I did not approach the chalet, but set out confidently on the wider path. The route ran between the snowdrifts higher on the mountain side than on the valley, but I saw also that now I was leaving the lights of the village behind, and this path, although easier to follow, was leading directly into a wood of pines above me. I came to a small grotto on the valley side of the slope, and beyond, a little further up on the mountain, I could see the white, stone façade of a closed church. A mound of snow nestling uneasily on the steep roof of the grotto slid off quietly in slow motion into my path, seconds before I reached it. Perversely I plundered on. This is the wrong way, I'm sure it is, I thought. More precious energy sapped by the extra effort of wading through the drift I came once more to a halt. The wind blew relentlessly. I noticed it for the first time. There is something noxious about the innocence of snow in its insidious transformation of familiar routes. I must go back. I turned and hurried back between the church and grotto, and reached, with a great deal of effort, the turning point on the path yet again. If I meet someone now will they be friend or foe? If I go to that chalet to ask will I be welcome? If I could somehow find the energy to climb further. I suddenly understood more perfectly than at any other moment that Fate, like a love affair, is a matter of timing: the right person passing at the right time; a combination of moments from experience which keep coming round like a memory, recurring, inducing in us the same confusion. It was as though I had stood all my life in the same cold place between the curtain and the glass. How stupid I am.

This whole journey is pointless, I said aloud to no one. I could have gone for the bus. I closed my eyes and breathed painfully.

"Where is Michael John, Ameldia? Why did you let him go? You're older, you should be more responsible! What bus? At what time?"

The conductor remembered him. He didn't have any money. No, he didn't put him off. On Christmas Day for thrupence? It wasn't worth it. He didn't remember when he got off. He hadn't seen him get off. There was a memorial service on the feast of the Purification; they waited and waited. There was no coffin, only flowers in the church, and my mother's tears all during the service. He went away so completely, he even went out of my dreams. Fair and small and mischievous.

When I opened my eyes a white mist was forming. I would have to hurry and get to the road before it enveloped me completely. Every step uphill was excruciatingly painful as again and again the skis bit into my shoulder. As I neared the top of the hill, passing through the farm smells, I heard voices. Two girls and a boy appeared, I went very slowly passing them higher up the slope; I had climbed very high. They took the downward path, several feet of snow separated us. They did not glance in my direction and I had lost my curiosity about the route. We passed in silence. I got to the road again where I started out, exhausted. Did anyone pass him that night and not know?

Once on the highway I walked more easily where the traffic of the day had beaten down the snowtrack. My alarm had evaporated like the mist on the mountain. But I was hungry and tired and when I reached the car-park where the ski bus turned it was deserted, no one was waiting. I put the skis into a bank of snow and lay against them. My face burned, and my hair clung to my forehead from the effort and panic of climbing. A car passed. It was too dark to read my watch. If I walked on to the road towards the lights I would be able to read the time. I was too tired to move. My shoulders ached. I could not lift my arms above my head. My clothes clung. The backs of my knees were damp. My leather gloves looked swollen and bloated. Another car passed. It must be late; perhaps he will come out looking for me. If I go and stand on the road he might see me. I was too weary to move, so I stayed on. Then a familiar throaty rattle of an engine sounded, and a bus turned into the coach-park.

"Mégève?"

"Non. Sallandes."

"Oh." I must have looked disappointed.

"Dix minutes!" he assured me.

"Oh. Merci, monsieur!" I brightened.

He was back in half the time to pick me up. I dropped my skis into the cage at the back and in a few minutes we were hurtling down the mountain towards the village.

At seven thirty I got to the hotel. Joe was not there. The X-rays from the clinic were lying on the bed. Perhaps he was worried and has gone out looking from me, I thought. I was drying my wet clothes on the radiators when he came in.

"What on earth happened?" I asked at the sight of the sling.

"Oh, some idiot got out of control and jumped on my back this afternoon. Arrogant lout. He didn't even apologize. He said I shouldn't have stopped suddenly in front of him."

"Why did you stop?"

"A girl in front of me fell down. I stopped to help her."

"It's dangerous though, isn't it. You should have skied round her to safety and then stopped."

"Well, anyway, I won't be able to ski again this holiday," he said. "The ligaments are torn."

"Is it very painful?"

"It's a bit sore."

"I'm sorry. Shall we go back tomorrow?"

"Well, we could go to Paris tomorrow instead of on Friday."

"Let's do that, I'll drive," I said.

"There's no need. I can manage. I have no trouble driving,"

he said. "How are you then, all right? Had a nice day?"

"Joe, I got lost on the mountain."

"Did you?" he said "Oh, by the way, I've been downstairs talking to Madame. I told her that we were leaving earlier. She was very sympathetic when she saw the sling. She said she wouldn't charge us for the extra nights even though we've booked to stay till Friday."

"I tried to walk down the path we skied on and then I couldn't find it."

"That was silly," he said. "Why didn't you get the bus?"

"I don't know."

It wasn't the first time in our ten-year relationship of living together and not living together that I found I had nothing to tell him. He never guessed the fury of my drama; and now he looked pale and tired.

"What's the matter?" he asked, catching me watching him.

"Nothing. Nothing's the matter."

Even in Montmartre there was snow and coldness.

"There's a hotel! Stop now!" I said.

We had been driving all day, yet it seemed as though we never left the snowline.

"Stop! Please. That hotel looked nice. Joe, I'm not navigating a street further."

"Ameldia, it's a five-star hotel!" he said, in a voice that reminded me of my mother. "We are not staying in a five-star hotel!"

"It's on me," I said extravagantly. "Whatever this costs, it's on me!"

"But Amee, you don't have any money!"

"I'll argue with the bank manager about that, not with you," I said. "I have a little plastic card here which will settle everything. Now will you get out of the car. Please Joe. You look exhausted!"

We signed into a fourth-floor side room. Through the nylon

45

curtains I could see the traffic of Paris and the lights of the Eiffel Tower. "We can walk to the Sacré Coeur from here. I think I remember the way," I said.

My last visit had been as a schoolgirl fifteen years before.

There were tangerines in the restaurant—I lifted my head to them as they passed on the fruit tray to the table next to us—and ice-cubes on the grapes. I shivered involuntarily. I don't remember satsumas any other year.

'I forgot to ring my mother on Christmas Day!" I said suddenly.

"From the French Alps? Why would you want to do that?" he said.

"You know what they're like about me being away for Christmas."

"No, I'm afraid I don't, I've never met them," he said firmly. "And I'm afraid I don't see why you think they should still be so obsessed with you. You are thirty years of age now, Ameldia, and you do have other brothers and sisters!"

"Yes, I know. But I was the only one around when—"

"Forget it!" he said "I didn't spend all this money and bring you all this way for you to drag that up now!"

"Madame? Monsieur?" A waiter stood eyeing us, his pencil poised like a dagger ready to attack his notepad.

Later as we passed through the square in Montmartre sad-eyed artists were putting their easels away. An African spread out ivory bangles and elephants on a cloth on the pavement and I stopped to admire. He spoke English: "Are you English?"

"No. Irlande."

"Ah. Irlande is good," he said, putting an arm around me and drawing me towards his wares. I felt like a schoolgirl again, shy, drawing away, explaining I had no money to buy anything.

Joe watched me from a distance and I said: "Don't be so grumpy."

"I'm not grumpy," he said crossly.

"Wouldn't it be nice to go and have a glass of wine in one of those bars," I said.

"Well, they look very crowded to me and I'm tired," he said.

"Do you know why I love Montmartre?"

"No, but I'm sure you're going to tell me!" he said.

"Because whatever time you come here, it's always open, full of people."

I wished I hadn't brought him to Montmartre. He seemed so uneasy amidst the haggle of trading in the streets. I had forgotten how he hated markets. He did not relax until we got back to the hotel.

I was not tired and didn't find that sleep came easily. My tossing and turning kept him awake.

"Where did you get that cough from?" he asked.

"I must have got cold somewhere."

I got up and went to the fridge for a glass of mineral water and as I opened the door in the dark, I thought I smelt oranges.

"Did you spill the fruit juice?" I asked.

"No," he said wearily. "When will you go to sleep?"

I went to the shower room to drink the water so as not to disturb him, and when I returned to the bedroom I found it was very much colder than when I'd left it. The curtain shifting slightly caught my attention. The glass in the window was so clear it looked as if it wasn't there at all.

"Joe?" I called softly. "Did you open the window?"

"No," he said without stirring.

The room appeared to be filling with a white mist. It's like on the mountain, I thought. The white mist of the night outside seemed to grow into the room.

"That's funny." The smell of oranges was very strong. "Somebody is eating satsumas!" I said aloud.

Joe didn't answer. I got into bed and lay down trembling. The walls of the room were gradually slipping away to the mist. "No. I will not watch," I said firmly. "I will not watch any more." I closed my eyes tight against the dark and breathed softly.

Where the white rocks of the Antrim Plateau meet the mud banks of the Lough, three small boys netting crabs dislodged a large stone, when one of them reaching into the water after the escaping crab caught instead the cold hand of my brother. In May, a closed coffin filled the sitting room and the Children of Mary from the neighbourhood came to pray there and keep the vigil.

"I will not watch," I said. "I will not watch."

An angel of Portland stone marked the grave and we sang: "Blood of my Saviour wash me in thy tide". "He was bound for heaven," my mother said often, and that seemed to console her. And every Sunday of the year we went to the cemetery, my mother and I; on Christmas Day ever after we left offerings of flowers and things until even the angelstone aged, became pockmarked and turned brown. It was the first Christmas I had not gone to that grave.

In the morning Joe drew back the curtains in the room and said: "What a sight! I'm glad I didn't know that was there last night."

"Didn't know what?" I said, moving to the window.

"Look!"

A huddle of stone crucifixes, headstones and vaults marked the graves which jostled for the space under our window against the side wall of the hotel.

"Montmartre cemetery!" he said.

There were no angels among the headstones.

"How creepy! Well, I'm glad we're going," he said, with a last glance before dropping the curtain.

But I could still see.

"Last night," I began to say, "this room was very cold and I asked you if—"

"Oh, do come away from that window and hurry up and pack," he said. "We need to catch the lunch-time ferry."

I wanted to tell him what I now knew, that the future was already a part of what I was becoming, and if I stopped this becoming there would be no future only an endless repetition of moments from the past which I will be compelled to relive. "It would help if you stopped breathing," he had said. But it wouldn't; because there would always be the memory of existence—like a snare; a trapped moment, hungover in the wrong time. Unaccountable. And I wanted to tell him before it was too late that the difference is as fragile between the living and the dead as the absence of breath on a glass. But already he was rushing on a journey to somewhere else.

Bound for heaven, was it? Yes. Hand and foot.

Naming the Names

Abyssinia, Alma, Bosnia, Balaclava, Belgrade, Bombay.

It was late summer—August, like the summer of the fire. He hadn't rung for three weeks.

I walked down the Falls towards the reconverted cinema: "the largest second-hand bookshop in the world", the billboard read. Of course it wasn't. What we did have was a vast collection of historical manuscripts, myths and legends, political pamphlets, and we ran an exchange service for readers of crime, western and paperback romances. By far the most popular section for which Chrissie was responsible, since the local library had been petrol bombed.

I was late when I arrived, the dossers from St Vincent de Paul hostel had already gone in to check the morning papers. I passed them sitting on the steps every working day: Isabella wore black fishnet tights and a small hat with a half veil, and long black gloves even on the warmest day and eyed me from the feet up; Eileen who was dumpy and smelt of meths and talcum powder looked at everyone with the sad eyes of a cow. Tom was the thin wiry one, he would nod, and Harry, who was large and grey like his overcoat, and usually had a stubble, cleared his throat and spat before he spoke. Chrissie once told me when I started working there that both of the men were in love with Isabella and that was why Eileen always looked so sad. And usually too Mrs O'Hare from Spinner Street would still be cleaning the brass handles and finger plates and waiting like the others for the papers, so that she could read the horoscopes before they got to the racing pages. On this particular day, however, the brasses had been cleaned and the steps were empty. I tried to remember what it had been like as a cinema, but couldn't. I only remember a film I'd seen there once, in black and white: *A Town like Alice*.

Sharleen McCabe was unpacking the contents of a shopping bag on to the counter. Chrissie was there with a cigarette in one hand flicking the ash into the cap of her Yves St Laurent perfume spray and shaking her head.

She looked up as I passed: "Miss Macken isn't in yet, so if you hurry you'll be all right."

She was very tanned—because she took her holidays early—and her pink lipstick matched her dress. Sharleen was gazing at her in admiration.

"Well?"

"I want three murders for my granny."

I left my coat in the office and hurried back to the counter as Miss Macken arrived. I had carefully avoided looking at the office phone, but I remember thinking: I wonder if he'll ring today?

Miss Macken swept past: "Good morning, ladies."

"Bang goes my chance of another fag before break," Chrissie said.

"I thought she was seeing a customer this morning."

Sharleen was standing at the desk reading the dust-covers of a pile of books, and rejecting each in turn:

"There's only one here she hasn't read."

"How do you know?"

"Because her eyes is bad, I read them to her," Sharleen said.

"Well there's not much point in me looking if you're the only one who knows what she's read."

"You said children weren't allowed in there!" she said pointing to the auditorium.

"I've just given you permission," Chrissie said.

Sharleen started off at a run.

"Popular fiction's on the stage," Chrissie called after her.

"Children! When was that wee girl ever a child!"

51

"Finnula, the Irish section's like a holocaust! Would you like to do something about it. And would you please deal with these orders."

"Yes, Miss Macken."

"Christine, someone's just offered us a consignment of Mills and Boon. Would you check with the public library that they haven't been stolen."

"Righto," sighed Chrissie.

It could have been any other day.

Senior: Orangeism in Britain and Ireland; Sibbett: Orangeism in Ireland and Throughout the Empire. Ironic. That's what he was looking for the first time he came in. It started with an enquiry for two volumes of Sibbett. Being the Irish specialist I knew every book in the section. I hadn't seen it. I looked at the name and address again to make sure. And then I asked him to call. I said I thought I knew where I could get it and invited him to come and see the rest of our collection. A few days later, a young man, tall, fair, with very fine dark eyes, as if they'd been underlined with a grey pencil, appeared. He wasn't what I expected. He said it was the first time he'd been on the Falls Road. I took him round the section and he bought a great many things from us. He was surprised that such a valuable collection of Irish historical manuscripts was housed in a run-down cinema and said he was glad he'd called. He told me that he was a historian writing a thesis on Gladstone and the Home Rule Bills, and that he lived in Belfast in the summer but was at Oxford University. He also left with me an extensive booklist and I promised to try to get the other books he wanted. He gave me his phone number, so that I could ring him and tell him when something he was looking for came in. It was Sibbett he was most anxious about. An antiquarian bookseller I knew of sent me the book two weeks later, in July. So I rang him and arranged to meet him with it at a café in town near the City Hall.

Naming the Names

He was overjoyed and couldn't thank me enough, he said. And so it started. He told me that his father was a judge and that he lived with another student at Oxford called Susan. I told him that I lived with my grandmother until she died. And I also told him about my boyfriend Jack. So there didn't seem to be any danger.

We met twice a week in the café after that day; he explained something of his thesis to me: that the Protestant opposition to Gladstone and Home Rule was a rational one because Protestant industry at the time—shipbuilding and linen—was dependent on British markets. He told me how his grandfather had been an Ulster Volunteer. I told him my granny's stories of the Black and Tans, and of how she once met de Valera on a Dublin train while he was on the run disguised as an old woman. He laughed and said my grandmother had a great imagination. He was fascinated that I knew so much history; he said he'd never heard of Parnell until he went to Oxford. And he pronounced "Parnell" with a silent "n", so that it sounded strange.

By the end of the month, the café owner knew us by sight, and the time came on one particular evening he arrived before me, and was sitting surrounded by books and papers, when the owner remarked, as the bell inside the door rang:

"Ah. Here's your young lady now."

We blushed alarmingly. But it articulated the possibility I had constantly been pushing to the back of my mind. And I knew I felt a sharp and secret thrill in that statement.

A few hours later, I stood on tiptoe to kiss him as I left for my bus—nothing odd about that. I often kissed him on the side of the face as I left. This time however I deliberately kissed his mouth, and somehow, the kiss went on and on and on; he didn't let me go. When I stepped back on to my heels again I was reeling, and he had to catch me with his arm. I stood there staring at him on the pavement. I stammered "goodbye" and walked off hurriedly towards the bus-stop. He stood on in the street looking after me—and I knew without turning round that he was smiling.

"Sharleen. *Murder in the Cathedral* is not exactly a murder story," Chrissie was saying wearily.

"Well, why's it called that then?"

"It's a play about—" Chrissie hesitated—"martyrdom!"

"Oh."

"This is just too, too grisly," Chrissie said, examining the covers. "Do they always have to be murders? Would you not like a nice love story?"

"She doesn't like love stories," Sharleen said stubbornly. "She only likes murders."

At that moment Miss Macken reappeared: "You two girls can go for tea now—what is that smell?"

"I can't smell anything," Chrissie said.

"That's because you're wearing too much scent," Miss Macken said. She was moving perfunctorily to the biography shelving, and it wasn't until I followed her that I became aware of a very strong smell of methylated spirits. Harry was tucked behind a newspaper drinking himself silly. He appeared to be quite alone.

"Outside! Outside immediately!" Miss Macken roared. "Or I shall have you forcibly removed."

He rose up before us like a wounded bear whose sleep we had disturbed, and stood shaking his fist at her, and, cursing all of us, Isabella included, he ran out.

"What's wrong with him?"

"Rejection. Isabella ran off with Tom this morning, and didn't tell him where she was going. He's only drowning his sorrows," Chrissie said. "Apparently they had a big win yesterday. Eileen told him they'd run off to get married. But they've only gone to Bangor for the day."

"How do you know this?"

"Eileen told Mrs O'Hare and she told me."

"What kind of supervision is it when you two let that man drink in here with that child wandering around?" Miss Macken said, coming back from seeing Harry off the premises.

We both apologized and went up for tea.

There was little on the Falls Road that Mrs O'Hare didn't know about. As she made her way up and down the road in the mornings on her way to work she would call in and out of the shops, the library, the hospital, until a whole range of people I had never met would enter my life in our tea room by eleven o'clock. I knew that Mr Quincey, a Protestant, from the library, had met his second wife while burying his first at the City Cemetery one Saturday morning. I knew that Mr Downey, the gatehousekeeper at the hospital, had problems with his eldest daughter and didn't like her husband, and I was equally sure that thanks to Mrs O'Hare every detail of Chrissie's emotional entanglements were known by every ambulance driver at the Royal. As a result, I was very careful to say as little as possible in front of her. She didn't actually like me. It was Chrissie she bought buns for at tea time.

"Oh here! You'll never guess what Mrs McGlinchy at the bakery told me—" she was pouring tea into cups, but her eyes were on us. "Wait till you hear—" she looked down in time to see the tea pouring over the sides of the cup. She put the teapot down heavily on the table and continued: "Quincey's being transferred to Ballymacarrett when the library's reopened."

"Och you don't say?"

"It's the new boss at Central—that Englishwoman. It's after the bomb."

"But sure that was when everybody'd gone home."

"I know but it's security, you know! She doesn't want any more staff crossing the peace line at night. Not after that young—but wait till you hear—he won't go!"

"Good for him."

"He says he's been on the Falls for forty years and if they

55

transfer him now they might as well throw the keys of the library into the Republican Press Centre and the keys of the Royal Victoria Hospital in after them."

"He's quite right. It's ghettoization."

"Yes, but it's inevitable," I said.

"It's not inevitable, it's deliberate," said Chrissie. "It's exactly what the crowd want."

"Who?"

"The Provos. They want a ghetto: the next thing they'll be issuing us with passes to come and go."

"Security works both ways."

"You're telling me."

After that Chrissie left us to go down to the yard to renew her suntan. Mrs O'Hare watched her from the window.

"She'd find the sun anywhere, that one." She turned from the window. "Don't take what she says too much to heart. She's Jewish, you know. She doesn't understand."

I was glad when she went. She always felt a bit constrained with me. Because I didn't talk about my love life, as she called it, like Chrissie. But then I couldn't. I never really talked at all, to any of them.

The room overlooked the rooftops and back yards of West Belfast.

Gibson, Granville, Garnet, Grosvenor, Theodore, Cape, Kasmir.

Alone again I found myself thinking about the last time I had seen Jack. It was a long time ago: he was sitting at the end of the table. When things are not going well my emotions start playing truant. I wasn't surprised when he said:

"I've got an invitation to go to the States for six months."

I was buttering my toast at the time and didn't look up.

"I'm afraid I'm rather ambivalent about this relationship."

I started battering the top of my eggshell with a spoon.

"Finn! Are you listening?"

I nodded and asked: "When do you go?"

"Four weeks from now."

I knew the American trip was coming up.

"Very well. I'll move out until you've gone."

I finished breakfast and we spoke not another word until he dropped me at the steps of the bookshop.

"Finn, for God's sake! Get yourself a flat somewhere out of it! I don't imagine I'll be coming back." He said: "If you need any money, write to me."

I slammed the car door. Jack was always extremely practical: if you killed someone he would inform the police, get you legal aid, make arrangements for removing the body, he'd even clear up the mess if there was any—but he would never, never ask you why you did it. I'd thrown milk all over him once, some of it went on the floors and walls, and then I ran out of the house. When I came back he'd changed his clothes and mopped up the floor. Another time I smashed all the dinner dishes against the kitchen wall and locked myself in the bathroom, when I came out he had swept up all the plates and asked me if I wanted a cup of tea. He was a very good journalist, I think, but somehow I never talked to him about anything important.

Because Mrs Cooper from Milan Street had been caught trying to walk out with sixteen stolen romances in a shopping bag and had thrown herself on the floor as if having a heart attack, saying: "Oh holy Jay! Don't call the police. Oh holy Jay, my heart," Chrissie forgot to tell me about the phone call until nearly twelve o'clock.

"Oh, a customer rang, he wanted to talk to you about a book he said he was after. Sibbett. That was it. You were still at tea." She said, "I told him we were open to nine tonight and that you'd be here all day."

For three weeks he hadn't rung. I only had to pick up the phone and ring him as I'd done on other occasions. But this time I hoped he would contact me first.

"Is something wrong?" Chrissie said.

"I have to make a phone call."

After that first kiss on the street, the next time we met I took him to the house, about ten minutes' walk from the park.

"When did you say your granny died?" he asked, looking with surprise around the room.

"Oh, ages ago. I'm not very good at dates."

"Well, you don't appear to have changed much since. It's as if an old lady still lived here."

He found the relics, the Sacred Heart pictures and the water font strange. "You really ought to dust in here occasionally," he said, laughing. "What else do you do apart from work in the bookshop?"

"I read, watch television. Oh, and I see Jack," I said quickly, so as not to alarm him.

"Good Lord. Would you look at that web; it looks like it's been there for donkeys!"

A large web attaching itself in the greater part to the geraniums in the window had spread across a pile of books and ended up clinging heavily to the lace curtains.

"Yes. I like spiders," I said. "My granny used to say that a spider's web was a good omen. It means that we're safe from the soldiers!"

"It just means that you never open the curtains!" he said, laughing. Still wandering around the small room he asked: "Who is that lady? Is she your grandmother?"

"No. That's Countess Markievicz."

"I suppose your granny met her on a train in disguise—as an old man."

"No. But she did visit her in prison."

He shook his head: "The trouble with you—" he began, then suddenly he had a very kind look in his eyes. "You're improbable. No one would ever believe me." He stopped, and began again. "Sometimes I think—" he tapped me on the nose—"you live in a dream, Finn."

And then he kissed me, and held me; he only complained that I was too quiet.

It was nine thirty when I left the building and shut it up for the night: Miss Macken had offered to drop me home as she was leaving, but I said I'd prefer to walk. There were no buses on the road after nine because a few nights before a group of youths had stoned a bus passing Divis flats, and the bus driver was hurt. The whole day was a torment to me after that phone call and I wanted to think and walk.

When I got to the park I was so giddy that I didn't care whether he came or not. My stomach was in a knot—and I realized it was because I hadn't eaten all day. The summer was nearly over—I only knew that soon this too would be over. I had kept my feelings under control so well—I was always very good at that, contained, very contained—so well, that I thought if he even touched me I'd tell him—Oh run! Run for your life from me! At least I didn't tell him that I loved him or anything like that. Was it something to be glad about? And suddenly there were footsteps running behind me. I always listened for footsteps. I'd walked all through those streets at night but I had never been afraid until that moment.

I suddenly started to run when a voice called out:

"Finn! Wait!" It was his voice.

I stopped dead, and turned.

We stood by the grass verge.

"Why didn't you ring me?" I asked, listlessly, my head down in case he saw my eyes.

"Because I didn't think it was fair to you."

"Fair?"

"Because, well—"

"Well?"

"I'm in England and you're here. It's not very satisfactory."

"I see."

"Look, there's something I should tell you. It's—Susan's

been staying with us for the last three weeks."

"I see."

I couldn't possibly object since we both were supposed to have other lovers, there was no possibility of either of us complaining.

"But we could go to your place now if you like."

I was weakening. He stooped to kiss me and the whole business began as it had started. He kissed me and I kissed him and it went on and on.

"I was just getting over you," I said, standing up.

"I didn't know there was anything to get over. You're very good at saying nothing."

And before I could stop myself I was saying: "I think I've fallen in love with you."

He dropped his head and hardly dared look at me—he looked so pained—and more than anything I regretted that statement.

"You never told me that before," he said.

"I always felt constrained."

He began very slowly: "Look, there is something I have to say now. I'm getting married at the end of the summer." And more quickly. "But I can't give you up. I want to go on seeing you. Oh don't go! Please listen."

It was very cold in the park. I had a piercing pain in my ear because of the wind. A tricolour hung at a jaunty angle from the top of the pensioner's bungalow, placed there by some lads. The Army would take it down tomorrow in the morning. The swings, the trees and grass banks looked as thoroughly careworn as the surrounding streets.

Lincoln, Leeson, Marchioness and Mary, Slate, Sorella and Ward.

I used to name them in a skipping song.

The park had been my playplace as a child, I used to go there in the mornings and wait for someone to lead me across the road, to the first gate. Sometimes a passer-by would stop and take my hand, but most times the younger brother of the family who owned the bacon shop would cross with me.

"No road sense!" my grandmother used to say. "None at all."

In the afternoon he would come back for me. And I remember—

"Finn, are you listening? You mustn't stop talking to me, we could still be friends. I love being with you—Finn!"

I remember standing in the sawdust-filled shop waiting for him to finish his task—the smooth hiss of the slicing machine and the thin strips of bacon falling pat on to the greaseproof paper.

I began to walk away.

"Finn. I do love you." He said it for the first time.

I pulled up the collar of my coat and walked home without looking back.

It should have ended before I was so overcome with him I wept. And he said: What's wrong and took me and held me again.

It should have ended before he said: "Your soul has just smiled in your eyes at me—I've never seen it there before."

Before. It should have ended before. He was my last link with life and what a way to find him. I closed my eyes and tried to forget, all vision gone, only sound left: the night noises came.

The raucous laughter of late-night walkers; the huddle of tomcats on the backyard wall: someone somewhere is scraping a metal dustbin across a concrete yard; and far off in the distance a car screeches to a halt: a lone dog barks at an unseen presence, the night walkers pause in their walk past—the entry. Whose is the face at the empty window?—the shadows cast on the entry wall—the shape in the darkened doorway—the steps on the broken path—who pulled that curtain open quickly—and let it drop?

I woke with a start and the sound of brakes screeching in my ears—as if the screech had taken on a human voice and called my name in anguish: Finn! But when I listened, there was nothing. Only the sound of the night bells from St Paul's tolling in the distance.

I stayed awake until daybreak and with the light found some peace from dreams. At eight o'clock I went out. Every day of summer had been going on around me, seen and unseen, I had drifted through those days like one possessed.

Strange how quickly we are reassured by ordinariness: Isabella and Tom, Harry and Eileen, waiting on the steps. And Mrs O'Hare at the counter with her polishing cloth, and Miss Macken discussing her holiday plans with Chrissie. Externally at least, it could have been the same as the day before, yesterday—the day before I left him in the park. But I saw it differently. I saw it in a haze, and it didn't seem to have anything to do with me.

"The body was discovered by bin-men early this morning," Miss Macken said. "He was dumped in an entry."

"Oh, Finn, it's awful news," said Chrissie, turning.

"It's the last straw as far as I'm concerned," Miss Macken said.

"Mr Downey said it's the one thing that turned him—he'll not be back to the Royal after this."

"We knew him," Chrissie said.

"Who?"

"That young man. The one who looked like a girl."

"The police think he was coming from the Falls Road," Miss Macken said.

"They said it was because he was a judge's son," said Chrissie.

"The theory is", said Miss Macken, "that he was lured there by a woman. I expect they'll be coming to talk to us."

"Aye, they're all over the road this morning," said Mrs O'Hare.

"Where are their bloody black flags today?" said Chrissie
with tears in her eyes. "Where are their bloody black flags
today?"

At lunch time they came.

"Miss McQuillen, I wonder?"

A noisy row between Isabella and Eileen distracted me—
Eileen was insisting that Isabella owed her five pounds.

"Miss McQuillen, I wonder if you wouldn't mind answering
a few questions?"

"How well did you know . . . ?"

"When did you last see him?"

"What time did you leave him?"

"What exactly did he say?"

"Have you any connections with . . . ?"

Osman, Serbia, Sultan, Raglan, Bosnia, Belgrade, Rumania,
Sebastopol.

The names roll of my tongue like a litany.

"Has that something to do with Gladstone's foreign policy?"
he used to laugh and ask.

"No. Those are the streets of West Belfast."

Alma, Omar, Conway and Dunlewey. Dunville, Lady and
McDonnell.

Pray for us. (I used to say, just to please my grandmother.)
Now and at the hour.

At three o'clock in the afternoon of the previous day, a man I
knew came into the bookshop. I put the book he was selling on
the counter in front of me and began to check the pages. It was
so still you could hear the pages turn: "I think I can get him to
the park," I said.

Eileen had Isabella by the hair and she stopped. The
policeman who was writing—stopped.

Miss Macken was at the counter with Chrissie, she was

frowning—she looked over at me, and stopped. Chrissie suddenly turned and looked as well in my direction. No one spoke. We walked through the door on to the street.

Still no one spoke.

Mrs O'Hare was coming along the road from the bread shop, she raised her hand to wave and then stopped.

"Quickly," the policeman said. "Headquarters. Turn the car."

"But we're due in Hastings Street at two," his driver said.

"Do as I say."

Harry had just tumbled out of the bookies followed by Tom. They were laughing. And they stopped.

We passed the block where the babyclothes shop had been, and at the other end the undertakers: everything from birth to death on that road. Once. But gone now—just stumps where the buildings used to be—stumps like tombstones.

"Jesus. That was a thump in the stomach if ever I felt one," one policeman said to the other.

Already they were talking as if I didn't exist.

There were four or five people in the interview room.

A policewoman stood against the wall. The muscles in my face twitched. I put my hand up to stop it.

"Why did you pick him?"

"I didn't pick him. He was chosen. It was his father they were after. He's a judge."

"They?"

"I. I recognized the address when he wrote to me. Then he walked in."

"Who are the others? What are their names?"

"Abyssinia, Alma, Balaclava, Balkan."

"How did you become involved?"

"It goes back a long way."

"Miss McQuillen. You have a captive audience!"

"On the fourteenth of August 1969 I was escorting an English journalist through the Falls: his name was Jack McHenry."

"How did you meet him?"

"I am coming to that. I met him on the previous night, the thirteenth; there was a meeting outside Divis flats to protest about the police in the Bogside. The meeting took a petition to Springfield Road police station. But the police refused to open the door. Part of the crowd broke away and marched back down to Divis to Hastings Street police station and began throwing stones. There was trouble on the road all night because of roaming gangs. They stoned or petrol bombed a car with two fire chiefs and burned down a Protestant showroom at the bottom of Conway Street. I actually tried to stop it happening. He was there, at Balaclava Street, when it happened. He stopped me and asked me if I'd show him around the Falls. He felt uneasy being an Englishman and he didn't know his way around without a map. I said I'd be happy to."

"Were you a member of an illegal organization?"

"What organization? There were half a dozen guns in the Falls in '69 and a lot of old men who couldn't even deliver the *United Irishman* on time. And the women's section had been disbanded during the previous year because there was nothing for them to do but run around after the men and make the tea for the Ceilies. He asked me the same question that night, and I told him truthfully that I was not—then.

"On the evening of the fourteenth we walked up the Falls Road, it was early, we had been walking around all day, we were on our way back to his hotel—the Grand Central in Royal Avenue—he wanted to phone his editor and give an early report about events on the road. As we walked up the Falls from Divis towards Leeson Street, we passed a group of children in pyjamas going from Dover Street towards the flats. Further up the road at Conway Street a neighbour of ours was crossing the road to Balaclava Street with his children; he said he was taking them to Sultan Street Hall for the night. Everything seemed quiet. We walked on down Leeson Street and into town through the Grosvenor Road: the town centre was quiet too. He phoned his paper and then took me to dinner to a Chinese restaurant across the road from the hotel. I remember it because there was a false ceiling in the restaurant, like a sky with fake star constellations. We sat in a velvet alcove and there were roses on the table. After dinner we went back to his hotel and went to bed. At five o'clock in the morning the phone rang. I thought it was an alarm call he'd placed. He slammed down the phone and jumped up and shouted at me: 'Get up quickly. All hell's broken loose in the Falls!'

"We walked quickly to the bottom of Castle Street and began to walk hurriedly up the road. At Divis Street I noticed that five or six shops around me had been destroyed by fire. At Divis flats a group of men stood, it was light by this time. When they heard that Jack was a journalist they began telling him about the firing. It had been going on all night they said, and several people were dead, including a child in the flats. They took him to see the bullet holes in the walls. The child was in a cot at the time. And the walls were thin. I left him there at Divis and hurried up the road to Conway Street. There was a large crowd there as well, my own people. I looked up the street to the top. There was another crowd at the junction of Ashmore Street—this crowd was from the Shankill—they were setting fire to a bar at the corner and looting it. Then some of the men began running down the street and breaking windows of the houses in Conway Street. They used brush handles. At the same time as the bar was burning, a number of the houses at the top of the street also caught fire in Conway Street. The crowd were throwing petrol bombs in after they broke the windows. I began to run up towards the fire. Several of the crowd also started running with me.

"Then I noticed for the first time, because my attention had been fixed on the burning houses that two turretted police vehicles were slowly moving down the street on either side. Somebody shouted: 'The gun turrets are pointed towards us!'

And everybody ran back. I didn't. I was left standing in the middle of the street, when a policeman, standing in a doorway, called to me: 'Get back! Get out of here before you get hurt.'

"The vehicles were slowly moving down Conway Street towards the Falls Road with the crowd behind them, burning houses as they went. I ran into the top of Balaclava Street at the bottom of Conway Street where our crowd were. A man started shouting at the top of his voice: 'They're going to fire. They're going to fire on us!'

"And our crowd ran off down the street again.

"A woman called to me from an upstairs window: 'Get out of the mouth of the street.' Something like that.

"I shouted: 'But the people! The people in the houses!'

"A man ran out and dragged me into a doorway. 'They're empty!' he said. 'They got out last night!' Then we both ran down to the bottom of Balaclava Street and turned the corner into Raglan Street. If he hadn't been holding me by my arm then that was the moment when I would have run back up towards the fires."

"Why did you want to do that? Why did you want to run back into Conway Street?"

"My grandmother lived there—near the top. He took me to Sultan Street refugee centre. 'She's looking for her granny,' he told a girl with a St John's Ambulance armband on. She was a form below me at school. My grandmother wasn't there. The girl told me not to worry because everyone had got out of Conway Street. But I didn't believe her. An ambulance from the Royal arrived to take some of the wounded to the hospital. She put me in the ambulance as well. It was the only transport on the road other than police vehicles. 'Go to the hospital and ask for her there,' she said.

"It was eight o'clock in the morning when I found her sleeping in a quiet room at the Royal. The nurse said she was tired, suffering from shock and a few cuts from flying glass. I stayed with her most of the day. I don't remember that she spoke to me. And then about six I had a cup of tea and wandered out on to the road up towards the park. Jack McHenry was there, writing it all down: 'It's all over,' he said. 'The Army are here.' We both looked down the Falls, there were several mills that I could see burning: the Spinning Mill and the Great Northern, and the British Army were marching in formation down the Falls road. After that I turned and walked along the Grosvenor Road into town and spent the night with him at his hotel. There was nowhere else for me to go."

I was suddenly very tired; more tired than on the day I sat in her room watching her sleep; more tired than on the day Jack left; infinitely more tired than I'd ever been in my life. I waited for someone else to speak. The room was warm and heavy and full of smoke. They waited. So I went on.

"Up until I met Jack McHenry I'd been screwing around like there was no tomorrow. I only went with him because there was no one else left. He stayed in Belfast because it was news. I never went back to school again. I had six O-levels and nothing else."

"Is that when you got involved?"

"No, not immediately. My first reaction was to get the hell out of it. It wasn't until the summer of '71 that I found myself on the Falls Road again. I got a job in the new second-hand bookshop where I now work. Or did. One day a man came in looking for something: 'Don't I know you?' he said. He had been a neighbour of ours at one time. 'I carried your granny out of Conway Street.' He told me that about eleven o'clock on the night of August fourteenth, there were two families trapped at the top of Conway Street. One of them, a family of eight, was escorted out of their house by a policeman and this man. Bottles and stones were thrown at them from a crowd at the top of the street. The policeman was cut on the head as he took the children out. The other family, a woman, with her two teenage daughters refused to leave her house because of her furniture. Eventually they were forced to run down the back entry into David Street to escape. It was she who told him that Mrs

McQuillen was still in the house. He went back up the street on his own this time. Because the lights in our house were out he hadn't realized there was anyone there. He got scared at the size of the crowd ahead and was going to run back when he heard her call out: "Finn! Finn!" He carried her down Conway Street running all the way. He asked me how she was keeping these days. I told him that she had recently died. Her heart gave up. She always had a weak heart.

"A few weeks later Jack took me on holiday to Greece with him. I don't really think he wanted me to go with him, he took me out of guilt. I'd rather forced the situation on him. We were sitting at a harbour café one afternoon, he was very moody and I'd had a tantrum because I found out about his latest girlfriend. I got up and walked away from him along the harbour front. I remember passing a man reading a newspaper at another café table, a few hundred yards along the quay. I saw a headline that made me turn back.

" 'The Army have introduced internment in Belfast,' I said.

"We went home a few days later and I walked into a house in Andersonstown of a man I knew: 'Is there anything for me to do?' I said. And that was how I became involved."

"And the man's name?"

"You already know his name. He was arrested by the Army at the beginning of the summer. I was coming up the street by the park at the time, when he jumped out of an Army Saracen and ran towards me. A soldier called out to him to stop, but he ran on. He was shot in the back. He was a well-known member of the Provisional IRA on the run. I was on my way to see him. His father was the man who carried my grandmother out of Conway Street. He used to own a bacon shop."

"Did Jack McHenry know of your involvement?"

"No. He didn't know what was happening to me. Eventually we drifted apart. He made me feel that in some way I had disappointed him."

"What sort of operations were you involved in?"

Anne Devlin

"My first job was during internment. Someone would come into the shop, the paymaster, he gave me money to deliver once a week to the wives of the men interned. The women would then come into the shop to collect it. It meant that nobody called at their houses, which were being watched. These were the old Republicans. The real movement was re-forming in Andersonstown."

"And the names? The names of the people involved?"

"There are no names. Only places."

"Perhaps you'll tell us the names later."

When they left me alone in the room I began to remember a dream I'd had towards the end of the time I was living with Jack. I slept very badly then, I never knew whether I was asleep or awake. One night it seemed to me that I was sitting up in bed with him. I was smoking, he was writing something, when an old woman whom I didn't recognize came towards me with her hands outstretched. I was horrified; I didn't know where she came from or how she got into our bedroom. I tried to make Jack see her but he couldn't. She just kept coming towards me. I had my back against the headboard of the bed and tried to fight her off. She grasped my hand and kept pulling me from the bed. She had very strong hands, like a man's, and she pulled and pulled and I struggled to release my hands. I called out for help of every sort, from God, from Jack. But she would not let go and I could not get my hands free. The struggle between us was so furious that it woke Jack. I realized then that I was dreaming. He put his hands on me to steady me: "You're having a fit. You're having a fit!" he kept saying. I still had my eyes closed even though I knew I was awake. I asked him not to let me see him. Until it had passed. I began to be terribly afraid, and when I was sure it had passed, I had to ask him to take me to the toilet. He never asked any questions but did exactly what I asked. He took me by the hand and led me to the bathroom where he waited with me. After that he took me back to bed again. As we

70

passed the mirror on the bedroom door I asked him not to let me see it. The room was full of mirrors, he went round covering them all up. Then he got into bed and took my hand again.

"Now please don't let me go," I said. "Whatever happens don't let go of my hand."

"I promise you. I won't," he said.

But I knew that he was frightened.

I closed my eyes and the old woman came towards me again. It was my grandmother; she was walking. I didn't recognize her the first time because—she had been in a wheelchair all her life.

She reached out and caught my hands again and the struggle between us began: she pulled and I held on. She pulled and I still held on.

"Come back!" Jack said. "Wherever you are, come back!"

She pulled with great force.

"Let go of me!" I cried.

Jack let go of my hand.

The policewoman who had been standing silently against the wall all the time stepped forward quickly. When I woke I was lying on the floor. There were several people in the room, and a doctor.

"Are you sure you're fit to continue?"

"Yes."

"What about the names?"

"My father and grandmother didn't speak for years: because he married my mother. I used to go and visit him. One night, as I was getting ready to go there, I must have been about seven or eight at the time, my grandmother said, 'Get your father something for his birthday for me'—she handed me three shillings—'but you don't have to tell him it's from me. Get him something for his cough.'"

"At the end of Norfolk Street was a sweet shop. I bought a tin of barley sugar. The tin was tartan: red and blue and green and black. They wrapped it in a twist of brown paper. I gave it to my

71

mother when I arrived. "It's for my Daddy for his birthday in the morning."

"From whom?"

"From me."

"Can I look?"

"Yes."

She opened the paper: "Why, it's beautiful," she said. I remember her excitement over it. "He'll be so pleased." She seemed very happy. I remember that. Because she was never very happy again. He died of consumption before his next birthday.

"Why did you live with your grandmother?"

"Because our house was too small."

"But the names? The names of the people in your organization?"

"Conway, Cupar, David, Percy, Dover and Divis. Mary, Merrion, Milan, McDonnell, Osman, Raglan, Ross, Rumania, Serbia, Slate, Sorella, Sultan, Theodore, Varna and Ward Street."

When I finished they had gone out of the room again. Only the policewoman remained. It is not the people but the streets I name.

The door opened again.

"There's someone to see you," they said.

Jack stood before me.

"In God's name, Finn. How and why?"

He wasn't supposed to ask that question. He shook his head and sighed: "I nearly married you."

Let's just say it was historical.

"I ask myself over and over what kind of woman are you, and I have to remind myself that I knew you, or I thought I knew you, and that I loved you once."

Once, once upon a time.

Naming the Names

"Anything is better then what you did, Finn. Anything! A bomb in a pub I could understand—not forgive, just understand—because of the arbitrariness of it. But—you caused the death of someone you had grown to know!"

I could not save him. I could only give him time.

"You should never have let me go!" I said, for the first time in ten years.

He looked puzzled: "But you weren't happy with me. You didn't seem very happy."

He stood watching for a minute and said: "Where are you, Finn? Where are you?"

And getting no answer he said: "May your God forgive you."

The door closed. An endless vista of solitude before me, of sleeping and waking alone in the dark—in the corner a spider was spinning a new web. I watched him move from angle to angle. An endless confinement before me and all too soon a slow gnawing hunger inside for something—I watched him weave the angles of his world in the space of the corner.

Once more they came back for the names, and I began: "Abyssinia, Alma, Balaclava, Balkan, Belgrade, Bosnia," naming the names: empty and broken and beaten places. I know no others.

Gone and going all the time.

Redevelopment. Nothing more dramatic than that: the planners are our bombers now. There is no heart in the Falls these days.

"But the names? The names of the people who murdered him? The others?"

"I know no others."

The gradual and deliberate processes weave their way in the dark corners of all our rooms, and when the finger is pointed, the hand turned, the face at the end of the finger is my face, the hand at the end of the arm that points is my hand, and the only account I can give is this: that if I lived for ever I could not tell: I could only glimpse what fatal visions stir that web's dark pattern, I do not know their names. I only know for certain what my part was, that even on the eve, on such a day, I took him there.

Ronald Frame

PICCADILLY PECCADILLOES
SECRETS
THE TREE HOUSE

Piccadilly Peccadilloes

She was fifty before her life really began. She'd made a lot of new friends since their move to Abinger. "Never mind forty," she'd tell them, making ripples in that quiet pool.

Only a certain amount was known about them in their new Surrey circles. Charles had retired from his job early, that much and no more was divulged: "FO. Foreign Office. Here, there and everywhere." (Someone even went to the bother of checking: it was all bona fide.) They had no children: "I don't think it's a life for them, not really, do you?" She said that coming here was just a beginning, she realized that her life after all their postings had many other possibilities left for her. (Other than what exactly, she didn't say in any more detail.) Her new friends nodded wisely when she added that now for the first time their lives were their own and naturally, having waited for it so long, she was going to make the most of it.

Her candour didn't altogether stop the speculation. It was her friends' opinion—and the reason why she attracted and kept them—that she lived very grandly for their means: she wasn't privy to these remarks, though, whispered rather guiltily after her lavish lunch parties had dispersed, and so happily she remained none the wiser. Of course they were right and wrong, her friends, as people always are about that kind of thing: top-flight Civil Service pensions aren't inexhaustible (there was more checking), but as she'd explained so often, for her it was like another life just beginning— "out of our grey period," she liked to say, making an arty joke of it.

At fifty, the magic age, she learned to drive. The other wives made do with rusty, hand-me-down Morris Minor Travellers, and brows furrowed when a high-performance, electric-blue Alfasud with fat tyres and black film-star windows appeared parked anyhow in front of the shops. "My gad-about," she called across to the warden, beaming at him and driving off before he had his slip completed.

The garage was informed through Mrs Perry that her husband wished to open an account; she told her confidantes she hated this sordid business of paying and having to appear knowledgeable about pumps and nozzles. She hinted they'd been used to things being done quite differently, she and Charles. The word got round later that it was the gardener's boy in the end who had to do the necessary. (The gardener's boy—two pairs of hands now in the garden—like the car and the front gate that swung back automatically and the sunken patio in the old rose garden, another extravagance much discussed of late in the more genteel domiciles of Abinger Hammer.)

Her favourite days, though, had nothing to do with Abinger or, properly, with Charles. "His golf's enough for him," she liked to say, making suffering faces.

No one saw much of Charles, least of all at the golf club: his port-wine nose and his jolly laugh collecting the papers in the morning had been welcome additions to the local scene when they came but all too little in evidence now, the husbands complained: too much of her and not enough of him. She repeated that she went to London only to get away from golf talk and locker-room jokes; so her lunch guests smiled with her and nodded because no one really knew positively what went on of an evening once the chintzy curtains were drawn across the creeper-fringed leaded windows. (Lunchtimes, oddly, were her social hour—a professional legacy, someone suggested vaguely —and Charles to the general disappointment declined many more invitations than he accepted.)

"Oh, yes. I need my lovely days up in London," she said very mysteriously. "Again." ("Again" in case her friends would forget she'd had another life before the one before.) She claimed it was an excuse to dress up: dress up *more*, she meant, because she'd set new standards for Abinger. "Treats keep you young." No one felt they could dispute the wisdom of *that*.

Two or three times a month it happened. She always took the Alfa. Driving gave her the illusion of somehow managing her own destiny. She parked at the underground car-park in Berkeley Square. Knightsbridge bored her now with its circus of tourists, wops hogging the pavements as if they bloody owned the place. "Horrids," she called the shop to her friends, who were impressed and shocked together by her occasional disrespect for seasoned customs.

After all those years away which she wouldn't be drawn on, she'd fallen into a routine surprisingly easily. Her morning began the way she liked it to begin, sipping a cup of coffee and eating a warm flaky croissant in the quiet of the Westbury Hotel coffee lounge. When she'd used the ladies' room she made a graceful exit through the front doors and headed straightaway for Bond Street.

She thought if anything *it* had improved with the years, unlike so much else. She sauntered up one side and down the other and remembered how she'd walked it with Charles in their salad days. She stopped at the windows, sighing at the pictures in her head till she felt they were starting to trouble her. She wouldn't let them trouble her. She had her favourite shops—The White House, Asprey's, Elizabeth Arden, Rayne—and she knew she'd only to walk inside any one of them to lose the memory. This was her own world. She felt she understood its magic. The names themselves were like a kind of spell. Pinet, Regine, Celine, Ferragamo.

She took her time and when she'd finished and seen all she wanted—perhaps even indulged herself in a pair of shoes or a silk square—she braved the traffic on Piccadilly and beetled off to Simpson's. She enjoyed telling her friends it was her favourite shop "absolutely anywhere". She loved its spaciousness and the cool white marble floors and stairs from an age she'd never known. When they were living in their backwaters she'd thought about it a lot; in Accra or Nicosia or Aden (she forgot which came before which) it had seemed to become everything she was being kept from. Now she could walk upstairs with her hand on the shiny steel and imagine she was Nancy Cunard or anyone else of that set with their mad, quicksilver lives she'd spent her years reading about. She loved lingering at the rails and she loved the shop's flattery of attention, the solicitous assistants scattered about each department anxious to help and no pains spared: that sort of service, like the décor, didn't seem to belong to this dismal age she'd come back to with its mania for sameness and impersonality. Sometimes she didn't want to leave and she'd spin the time out, choosing between one jumper and another or trying on the Daks skirts; the skirts had a clever way of making her look even thinner and narrower than she'd already disciplined herself to be.

After Simpson's it was lunchtime almost. She dropped into Hatchards and did a round of the fiction table and then quickly upstairs or downstairs according to her mood. She liked looking through the art books; just occasionally, though—it was against her better judgement, she felt—the intensity of the other people alarmed her slightly and then it was a relief to be back outside again on the street. Over-much intelligence was something she felt it prudent to be suspicious about.

At twelve fifteen she checked her watch and swept up the side stairs into the Ritz. The pink carpets and snowy marble always dazzled her till she could adjust to it. She sat on a stripy sofa in the bar and ordered a Tropical Dream. She fished two crisp pound notes out of her bag to include a tip. There was always the same handsome wavy-haired barman in a white apron, and she laid the two notes down separately on his tray. He'd started speaking to her the last few times, nice day, how was madam. She'd overheard his name was George. "I think that's a lovely name, so English," she ventured one day with a foreign lilt when the Tropical Dream seemed a stronger concoction than usual.

After the Ritz she stepped as nimbly as she could manage across Piccadilly in the direction of Stratton Street and Langan's Brasserie. She didn't like the indignity of being un-accompanied when the *maître* asked how many, but it was less galling than it might have been: it normally meant having to share a large round table for ones and twos which she actually found rather fun. She'd been lucky except once or twice, and she'd met some very interesting people. One came to face-spot of course, those she could after her years in the wilderness— she'd backed her chair into Michael Caine's ankles behind her once—but the table was fascinating in a different way. Catching up, she thought of it, if only to justify some of the expense. Rich Hampstead wives with lecherous gossip and sober-suited businessmen a little uncomfortable with the place and glamor-ous young people with frizzy hair smoking French cigarettes and discussing pop music. "I wonder what my Abinger friends would have to say to this?" she asked herself, and remembered timid, mousy wives she'd known in Nairobi and Penang. She effected means of either breaking into conversations or starting them: one lunch she was seated beside a rather fey young man who turned out to be a writer, and she told him she was a widow over from Switzerland on a spree. "I have to fit in Harley Street too. I was advised Lausanne for my arthritis. I was a painter of sorts. You won't remember. The best advice I ever had, Lausanne."

She liked to hear the black pianist and his Broadway classics, but sometimes the turbot or the artichoke missarda sat a little heavily in her stomach and she thought it better to get up and go. She'd lost the guilt of the first few times and confected appropriate excuses to suit the feel of the day: a meeting with my publisher, my jeweller's resetting some stones, I'm selling at Sotheby's, I've a recital tonight and I need the afternoon to rest.

Weighed down with her bags she moved stolidly off down Stratton Street and between the busy tides of pedestrians on Piccadilly. Soothed by the pianist's melodies she was ready to concentrate for a little while on something more cerebral. The Royal Academy was handy and rarely had anything she felt she didn't want to see: there were retrospectives of artists to rediscover and the summer shows and the big Chinese and Inca exhibitions. (She liked to say she was receptive to it all. "More or less. Everything except those awful piles of bricks and sand heaps they had in the *Telegraph*.") Occasionally the mental application proved itself just a little too much for her mid-afternoon frame of mind and she'd retreat more quickly than she usually allowed to Burlington Arcade. She'd walk the length of it twice, up and back, and then make her way back across Piccadilly and down Duke Street to the polite frenzy of Jermyn Street. She'd go into Dunhill, lured by the brown plush and low lights; she'd saunter round the cabinets, and the hush and the aisles would remind her what the shops used to be like in New York in the early sixties when Charles was still considered responsible enough to go. When she was done and beginning to tire she'd pop across the road to Fortnum's with the little energy left and into the Mezzanine for a seat and a pot of Keemun. She never bothered talking to anyone over tea. She bought odds and ends to take back: mustard for herself and jasmine tea ditto (Charles's taste buds had been the first thing to go), and maybe a tin of biscuits or a fruit cake would catch her eye and she'd start planning an afternoon tea around it.

The rest of her day passed without needing to think hardly. The tiredness crept up from her feet and she found there was just enough to do. Along to Burberry's, read the theatre and cinema bills, then the long stretch back to Berkeley Street. At five thirty, dead on her feet, she repaired to the Aloha Bar in the Mayfair Hotel and inaugurated the Happy Hour with something Hawaiian-sounding from the cocktail menu. Her thoughts always drifted to what she might do if she actually *were* a widow. Stay the night perhaps. Take a taxi to Swallow Street opposite Simpson's and order oysters and a good year's hock upstairs in Bentley's.

Thinking taxis put her in the mood and she informed the doorman and was speeded back to Berkeley Square in no time at all. It was much slower work driving up the ramps and out of the garage and around Berkeley Square to get to Mount Street, but she had the happiness of her day to divert her and she could even feel vaguely charitable to the other drivers around her. In the mirror waiting at the lights it would occur to her she looked younger than a woman of fifty-two with a not very easy life behind her, and thinking that she'd feel a slow glow warming inside her.

When she got home, of course, it was different. The gate swung back and she'd see from the other end of the drive he hadn't even drawn the curtains. She'd look in the mirror again to set her face properly before getting out. She'd reach into the boot for all her purchases and slam the lid shut to give him warning if he needed it. "If he can hear even, God help us."

Inside, every light in the house would be on. She'd find him eventually. The empty glasses and overturned bottles she remembered from a dozen other houses—tatty official residences and then the flats rented for them—would point the way. She'd right the bottles on the tables and patiently collect the glasses together by their stems, rubbing at wet circles on the polished wood with a paper handkerchief from her bag so the daily wouldn't notice. She could hear him usually, blundering about; sometimes he was sleeping; on the bad days the television would be on, turned up very loud, and she was grateful they'd never have neighbours again and all that over-polite hysteria of explaining in pidgin English.

Once she'd found him lying under the piano; another time he

was heaped up in the cupboard under the stairs. (Different, she reminded herself tartly, from oleander bushes.) Recently he'd taken to sprawling full-out on the window seat in the sitting room, a much more dangerous development. He wouldn't recognize her when she came in, and he could only tell who it was when he saw the familiar burden of carrier bags. She'd drop them on the sofa and come across and reach behind him and tug the curtains shut. If he looked as if he was going to suggest anything out of his stupor—what was it costing them, for Christ's sake—she'd kill him with a look.

She would carry on, calmly battering the cushions behind him into shape. She'd say something to pretend it had been a perfectly normal day for both of them. She'd see he was so drunk the words couldn't have come out anyway.

At some point when she was ready she'd begin her delicious little torture, opening her bags and emptying them on to the sofa. Shoes, jumper, blouse, skirt, scarf, books. Travel brochures were a new addition to her list, a glamorous world their missions had never taken them to: the French West Indies, Java, unpronounceable Pacific atolls.

Even if he found them in his soberer moments and could focus his eyes to read, she knew there'd be no serious objection raised. They had the situation, she now felt, understood. It was very simple, although it had taken them a dozen years getting there. So long as she said nothing about his own indulgences, he hadn't the moral authority to say anything about hers. Tit for tat. "My Piccadilly peccadilloes," she'd been telling her new friends, taking care they only saw one side of the coin.

She'd arrange her purchases over her arm to take them upstairs, leaving him crumpled with the words unsaid still muddling around in his head. Some day, she didn't doubt, he'd forget and try to say something. Then he'd get it back, what she'd been saving for twenty-five years and trailing round the shreds of the Commonwealth with her, he'd get it so hard he'd feel he'd been blown through the wall. It had never happened, and she hoped it wasn't ever going to. One couldn't be too sure, though. She lived these days on red alert.

They would finish the scene in the same way. She'd stop at the door on her way out and tell him she was tired and could he get himself something to eat. She would explain what there was and where. He never heard, but it was how she was playing it and meant to carry on. Till the alarm bells rang. She'd pause in the hall where he could see, angling her reflection in the mirror. She wondered what he thought, the worst he imagined of her seeing her slim and youthful still: if he drank what he did to tell himself it didn't matter.

"Well, then. Goodnight." She'd turn her back on him. She didn't waste time waiting for a reply she knew wasn't going to come. Pulling herself upstairs with her heavy armload of clothes, she was prey to a fleeting moment of doubt. It was just the tiredness of the day, but it was as if the walls were moving in on them and they'd water for air. Sometimes she felt a panic of little bubbles in her throat.

She'd pass herself in the wavy landing mirror. She never looked the same upstairs: suddenly she became grim and tight-mouthed. Her skin sagged in strange places. Fifty-two, she'd remind herself, and in front of her she'd see a person turned all to hate.

Secrets

He suspected it was his stomach, but even his doctor didn't seem very sure. He'd kept it from Hilary for as long as he could, but she'd noticed and would ask him in her vague way, why didn't he go to see someone else, a specialist? Whenever he tripped over the word "ulcer" in a book or a newspaper a kind of despair went through him.

He recorded some letters for the rota secretaries and left the others in the department with their instructions. In the car he felt the usual relief to be out of the building and away from it all, the bright steel and chrome and the Japanese gravel gardens and the rubber plants infesting their floor like a jungle. Someone had shown him a recent copy of *Design* with a feature on well-planned offices, including their own, and his eyes had started to glaze over as he read it.

He took the B-roads back. He hated the obligation of the dual carriageway and had begun to avoid it. This afternoon he was almost enjoying the strange quiet. He told himself it just needed a very minor dislocation like this to be seeing things through new eyes. It was a different race even, passing the cars on the network of humpback lanes after Gerrards Cross, housewives in headscarves picking children up from school, elderly couples in polished Rovers returning from the shops.

At conferences people eyed him a little askance when they asked him where he was from, and he said Buckinghamshire. Beaconsfield, he would add, and the eyes would narrow back at him. In a way, of course, it wasn't one thing or the other, he knew that: a red-tiled, whitewashed compromise marooned

mid-point between country and town. He wondered sometimes how he could explain to them that, really, he was satisfied,
perfectly content with the pretty painted shutters and the
cobbled walks and the wistaria-hung front their overgrown
village smiled on the world. Maybe it *is* a soft option, he wanted
to say, but Hilary and I, we're both of us quite happy.

There'd been a time certainly when the very same sort of
place would have seemed below his consideration—but only
because it was so far beyond his expectations. In the
old-fashioned parlance he could respect and understand, he'd
married above himself. He'd work it into the conversation that
Hilary's father still farmed in his Cotswold valley, breeding
horses. To get where *he'd* wanted to go all those years ago, he'd
had to disinherit himself—at the time the indeterminate mists of
suburbia hadn't seemed to him a real background at all—and,
he could have added, that's something you don't forget. When
he was wooing Hilary, he'd tell her confidently, hoping her
father might overhear them, "I'm never going back there
again."

Another ten years on and here they were, in not so dissimilar
territory. He wouldn't have been able to account for it if he'd
been asked what had gone wrong in his calculations. Not
"wrong" exactly, and not any one thing, he might have said: it's
only what happens to so many people, one's life seems to be
fitting certain conditions. Beaconsfield assimilated them both:
the prices were on the up and up, they'd delicatessens and wine
bars on Saturday for lunch, Volvos on either side of them. Their
neighbours lived decently and weren't ashamed of their quiet
affluence. He felt safe.

The knife twisted again in his stomach and he had to
pull into the side and rest for a few moments. In the mirror
he watched his eyes clouding and the sweat breaking on his
cheeks. Hilary, he reminded himself, concentrating on the
thought, wasn't to know anything. If she ever chanced to
find out . . . His mind wandered, but the possibilities always

frightened him so much he told himself "no" and just let it go.

It was a naïvely sentimental thing to think, but it was true: he'd meant everything in his life for Hilary.

They'd met at a hunt ball in Cirencester. When he was at Oxford he'd picked up a curious set of friends: acquaintances rather than friends. Scientists from Surbiton weren't their usual company, and he'd never got beyond the fringes of their coteries, however hard he applied himself. He didn't know enough people in his own right and he could never be drawn on his background—it would have been damnation for anyone else—but he'd been tolerated: his looks appealed to both sexes for all sorts of reasons, and learning from that he'd quickly developed the knack of anticipating a person's likes and dislikes and being just that bit more voluble in his criticisms than the rest of the company would allow themselves to be. He was hauled along to hunt balls and point-to-points and regattas and rooftop parties because he could be guaranteed to come up with the withering line, the loud aside, that was going to send the occasion up mercilessly and no one to blame but himself. He bought beige cords and heavy brogues and high-buttoning hacking jackets so that when people asked him what he did and he told them the truth—engineering—they'd look a little hesitant and then laugh, seeing it must be another joke.

Hilary, statuesque and handsome and with so strangely little to say for herself, had been just as uncertain, never seeming to know any better where she was with him. In spite of it, though—or because of it—their love had prospered. On weekends he would take the bus to Astalleigh and spend Saturday night at the farm, adjusting himself quietly to those spacious low-beamed rooms with their ticking clocks and chintz sofas and blue-and-white bowls of pot pourri. Hilary with her empty days became his intimate contact with a lulling, more perfect world, and he came to think of her more and more as its personification and was duly grateful.

He'd also known what he knew now, that it wasn't quite as simple as that. Then, like now, there were things they wouldn't touch on, presumably because they'd wanted it like that. She'd been like a charm for him and he was happier than he'd been in his life before, and knowing any more than he had might have been confusing things needlessly, willing the spell not to hold.

She'd let him know when he first came calling that there were other men who had prior claims to his. Even later, she'd never contrived to conceal that from him. He used to watch them careering down to the farm in their Land Rovers or catch glimpses of her on a day out in Oxford whistling past in a red Spitfire. He'd been walking past the windows of the Randolph's cocktail bar once and seen her on a stool sipping a long drink with a moustached young man who was biting the cherry off the end of her swizzle stick.

She'd had any number of offers—she told him how many—and in the end she'd chosen him. He'd never been able to decide why. Speculating about it even was like analysing his luck, and he gave up. Her father, with his countryman's accidental instinct for shams, had seen through him and detached himself. His degree when the time came couldn't have cut much ice; even Hilary's pride was smothered in indecipherable smiles. It used to console him that her mother was so agreeable: she'd wanted her youngest daughter to grow up cultured and couldn't believe anything else of her, although it was patently clear to the rest of her circle that it was less than the truth. He'd wondered long after, perhaps she'd understood what they couldn't, that the idea of his learning and his social mobility too, both combined, and her daughter's virtues, the practical wisdom of her boarding school—tapestry roses on stale afternoons, long letters to her nephews and nieces to while away the evenings in the fragrant sitting room—the two somehow, by a natural affinity, belonged together.

Ten years later, with the past still unsolved, he'd knowledge

enough of them both to know that at least she couldn't become
any less to him. She still wore her refinement lightly, reminding
him of Astalleigh, breathing it through their rooms like perfume
trails on the air. He told people she had the instincts and the
little touches he'd never had. He watched her, never tiring of
the spectacle: the way she held her knife and fork, the tilt of her
wrist when she drank tea, an authority transported by her whole
body just crossing a room. Linen napkins in silver rings,
walking sticks in the hall, the loo paper cut into single sheets in a
bamboo tray.

All that, their intimates were meant to deduce, had been *her*
contribution over the years. They could see too he had the sort
of pride that meant offering something back in equal measure.
It was a talking point among their few choice friends that, even
before he was taken on to the company board, he would spend
every penny he earned and it was all for Hilary.

They were seeing it, of course, from the outside. A Georgian
six-legged sideboard, two Sickert sketches, a cabinet of
Venetian glass, in their hall a walnut console table with a marble
top. On the other side of the baize-lined front door, if they could
have known, things worked themselves out with equal civility
and the same tasteful understatement.

Hilary happened to say one day she wished they were able to
entertain more people, and the next few weeks were taken up
plying the antiques shops till they found an oval Queen Anne
table that gatelegged so that they could lay ten places if she
wanted. They realized they must have chairs for their guests.
They found a set of twelve with shield backs and needle-point
seats at a manor house sale and continued bidding till they were
theirs. He bought her presents of blue-and-white Chinese bowls
and she filled them without his ever needing to say anything (the
pot pourri, she announced, came ready-made from a garden
centre in High Wycombe). He instigated things which he knew
would please her but which would have required too much

concentration for her attention if he'd left it to her to decide: in the past couple of years he'd taken out a second mortgage on a cottage clamped to a cliffside near Tintagel, he'd sold her runabout as a surprise and bought her a high-performance Scirocco with tinted windows and a rival firm's stereo system. She responded to his concern when he told her that he was happy if she was happy. She mentioned one evening she'd always wanted to paint and the next morning he arranged that an art shop would deliver everything she needed, and when she said she'd like to go on a painter's holiday on her own he told her "of course" and talked her into taking the most expensive. Her itinerary included Provence and the Italian lakes and they drove up to London together and bought a suitcaseful of lightweight clothes in Liberty's and Simpson's. Of late she had declared abstracts were beginning to appeal to her, and he'd surveyed the drawing-room walls wondering on the possibilities. She informed him there was a gallery in Grafton Street which specialized and he'd phoned up and blanched in the office window when they gave him a sample of their prices.

Needless to say, he couldn't have done it merely on the salary he was paid. He couldn't understand if *she* understood that or if his behaviour from the outset had somehow convinced her that he really could afford it.

His stomach tightened again, there was another wrench as the knife twisted deeper. It was inevitable, he told himself, turning back into the side of the road. He'd begun to suspect they were on to him. It was only a matter of time, anyway. He could think he was like a barometer when it came to people's feelings. He'd already caught the climatic shifts starting among his colleagues, the very slight evasions calculated not to offend, the holdings-back barely perceptible to an uninformed eye.

Five years before, the company, holding to his advice on market trends, had inaugurated its research on a new range for the eighties—videotape recorders one-third the bulk and weight of their originals, a stereo cassette player that could be fitted into a pocket. He'd studied Japanese developments in microchip technology and the latest simultaneous project was a compendium of video games the size of a slim paperback. The firm was sinking everything it could into his research department, but he'd sometimes wondered if it would ever be enough. Occasionally he would worry about it. Hilary had never expressed any interest in his work and would let any comments he let slip pass her by. He'd immediately regret having said anything, and she'd smile serenely when he apologized as if the offence hadn't even registered.

At some point over the five years, by some accident—he'd forgotten when or how: at a conference perhaps—he'd met someone from one of the American giants. They'd had a profitable discussion—and then another, which considered their shared interests further, and then another one after that. He let them pay for a holiday in New York, which Hilary had loved for its violent, vulgar contrasts to everything she'd been used to. They had another holiday at Christmas time in Palm Beach with one of the executives and his tanned society wife.

It was never directly suggested that he should enter their employ, either officially or unofficially. There'd been some necessary skullduggery late one summer's afternoon in the cocktail bar of the Westbury Hotel which had been a little too furtive for his comfort—something to do with an unmarked envelope and the equivalent of four months' salary—but he could convince himself that had only been intended as an expression of trust and appreciation from his American correspondents, and he'd accepted it with the sincerity which seemed owing and with the simple grace he imagined Hilary might have conferred on the occasion.

The two of them began to frequent the Westbury on their visits to London. Hilary seemed unthinkingly at home in the muted good taste of their room, watching from the window the elegant life passing on Conduit Street, never questioning what it meant, how it was they could support this life. He made journeys up he didn't tell her about, meeting his contact (it would be someone different every time) in restaurants in Hampstead or Highgate preselected for them because they were well off the usual business-account circuit. He gave his new associates what experience was instructing him merited a fair price, and he began holding out till he felt he'd got it. He hated the physical act of handing the papers over, the anonymous buff envelopes which his table companions seemed able to slip into their slimline cases with a sort of professional ease, even managing a laugh as they snapped the lock shut. Afterwards, like a penance, he'd stop off at Harrods and buy Hilary something in the parfumerie—an expensive fragrance like Worth or Amazone or Diorissimo, it didn't really matter which: he'd taught her to like them, but he still hadn't learned to tell them apart—and then he'd take the motorway back, winging home in fifth, filling the car with radio voices to kill the thoughts hammering in his head.

Recently he'd caught the news coming through about the Americans and an ambitious new sales programme they were supposed to be launching: attractions included a miniaturized video deck with a compendium of games on recall and a stereo cassette player lightweight and neat enough to be carried around in a pocket. He'd been busy the last few weeks assuring everyone it didn't mean anything: "Stories get about. You know how it is. Talk big, and people are going to believe you." He'd smile encouragingly round the department as he exited early for another consultation with the doctor in Chalfont St Giles.

The four years were beginning to tell on him. He saw it in people's expressions, the concern and caution confused. Faces watched him from the windows as he drove out of the car-park and fixed the white Mercedes like an electric toy on the right track home.

On those bad days when he was living in his stomach, he'd try

93

to think of Hilary. Sentimental thoughts. He'd remind himself
she was the one constant left, still the woman he'd had such
youthfully passionate desires to make his own. He would have
the familiar sense too that it wasn't, never had been, quite like
that. Facts, his reason would insist, needed to be faced. Facts
like having lived their days without each other for ten years and
knowing that their evenings after the formal dinner that had
been such a novelty once couldn't bring them very much closer
again. Himself reading or listening to music while Hilary
scribbled letters to girlhood friends or painted noiselessly
overhead in her loft. On their weekends dressing elegantly,
doing Beaconsfield things, eating out, walking in green
gumboots with the dogs through silent woods twenty yards
apart.

It wasn't everything. He'd tell himself no, it wasn't
everything, but it was enough, and more than most people could
expect of their lives. It was the intangible things she was the
catalyst for which persuaded him in the end that they lived and
loved by a special kind of alchemy that set them apart. The elixir
was the aura of graciousness she carried about with her—
graciousness, good taste, sensibility, refinement—speaking it in
her choice, low-pitched Cheltenham Ladies' College vowels,
trailing it through the rooms like her expensive Harrods
perfumes he couldn't tell apart. It concerned him very
occasionally that he had to lie to her about the lunch trips: it
came to matter less and less that what he was dealing in were
company secrets, what slightly disturbed him was a double-deal
on that which might have been playing on her trust. Might have
been—if he hadn't known her better, felt the coldness from her
when he mentioned work.

To comfort himself he'd try remembering all the things he'd
bought to give her virtues a perfect and seemly home. The
means had now ceased to interest him. Even the physical
discomfort in a way was part of the sacrifice. Driving home he'd
forget the pain drilling inside: in his head he was surprising

Hilary's sculptured dignity as he surprised it every night, catching her mid-sentence on the phone, in the kitchen grandly shaking a lettuce dry, sipping Dubonnet Dry at the window and watching the shadows lengthen in the garden. He lived for the secret link that held the pieces together, locked them into place—Hilary's slow turn-around, the quiet smile, her patience as he touched her lips with his, her approval with him he could feel without hearing it explained in helpless words. It had been the reason why and the justification for it and his reward that made any price seem worth paying.

He had about a hundred yards to go.

A bonfire wafted smoke over a beech hedge. A hired gardener whirred a Flymo over the Scottish lady's verge. The Tresanton girl had some friends in on the tennis court and he heard their light, trilly laughs.

He'd turned the corner before he saw the car outside the house, tucked up against the verge. He didn't recognize it and made rapid calculations whose and why. He felt detonations in his stomach. He only wanted to be home, safe inside.

He stopped on the other side of the road to give whoever it was a minute or two. He drummed his fingers along the rim of the steering wheel. He was thinking it must be someone for one of their neighbours and was looking at the house for clues when he saw Hilary moving behind the upstairs landing window. His fingers were on the ignition key when he caught another movement and he saw she wasn't alone.

It was hard to tell at first, but he knew it was a man before his eyes could be quite sure.

He couldn't see all of him, the window cut off some of his height. Hilary had her hand on the banister rail and stopped and turned back. The figures for a moment crossed, held still.

His eyes couldn't cope and dropped to the road, the verge, his fingers tightening on the wheel. He could feel the pain drilling deeper, excavating through the lining of his stomach, tempting the unknown. He closed his eyes on it.

He opened them again as the first wave passed and he saw everything exactly the same, the yellow car, the road curving ahead, the cropped verge rising to the beech hedge, the outside of the house. He looked at the house more closely than he'd looked for a very long time. He wanted all the details. He saw the cottagey pretensions he'd forgotten about, the arched oak door and the tiled steps and the rainbarrel and the powder blue shutters and the tiny upstairs windows in the high, steeped roof like eyes watching back, slyly considering.

He lifted the handbrake and let the car gently freewheel past the house towards the corner. Ten minutes, quarter of an hour he'd give them. He'd come back and it would be all over, the car would have gone. He'd sweep into the half-moon of driveway and there would be the crunch of gravel, the chips spinning beneath the wheels. Not the same contained explosion he always listened for, the comforting sounds of journey's end. Something told him there was another journey just about to begin.

He rolled past the other houses on the avenue. His head felt very light and free and apart from all the rest of him. He imagined it tipping itself out, shaking the bits loose.

He slowed down passing the back of the Tresantons' and watched for white movements through the hedge. He lowered the window for some air and listened to the balls being flung over the net on tight racquets. On summer evenings he liked to listen from the garden for the solace of those dependable returns, plung—plung—plung. He came down on the brake, waiting for the end of the rally and then the round of schoolgirl giggles.

At the junction he took the Beaconsfield road. He'd left a reserve in an antiques shop on a Ming countryware bowl. It would put the time off. He'd go back in and say, thank you, no, he didn't think so, it wasn't quite . . . The man who owned the shop would smile at him, shrug his shoulders. "You're a valued customer, Mr Elverson. It's my pleasure. We'll have something else, I'm sure, before too long. Have a look round, please do, we've some other things."

He doubted if he could even pretend an interest, just this one particular afternoon of his life. He turned off before he reached the shop and took another side road back up towards the woods. He looked at his watch. He'd try doing a circle.

He concentrated on the red road. He asked the question, but why like this, suddenly so calm? The answer came easily to him, because I've never really known anyway. Realizing the vastness of his ignorance, like a vision of the blackness of space, he understood that confused with the despair there was some comfort too in these things. It had something to do with not thinking too deeply. He had never even considered, so why should he begin now? It was too late for beginnings: the eleventh hour and the fifty-ninth minute.

He told himself, safe with our secrets.

The road opened out in front of him, making a long run up to the lowering copse of trees at the top of the hill. At its core, where he couldn't see, a pit of darkness beckoned, it seemed to be drawing him . .

He changed gear and brought his foot down on the accelerator. The engine growled and he felt the months begin to lift from him as the wheels bit the road hard and the first shudders shot through him.

The Tree House

They were walking down Drayton Gardens, the two of them. I
saw them from the other side of the road and stood behind a tree
tying my shoelace till they'd passed. I was perched on one leg,
shaking. They disappeared into a block of mansion flats.

I crossed the road and watched the windows from behind
another tree. The lights went on in a room in one of the middle
floors. She walked over to the balcony doors and looked out. He
was pouring drinks at the sideboard: I could just see the tops of
an armada of bottles. He handed her a glass and she took it
without looking at him. Maybe he put music on because she
started moving her hips. She was still watching the length of the
street. Could she have seen me? But if she was hoping for
another look to confirm it really had been me, she gave up soon
enough. She pivoted on her high heels, swinging round in her
silks to give herself to whatever domestic life they lived now like
tamed savages in the quiet heart of Chelsea.

We were children together once. There was Alan—and
Claire—and me. I think Alan—and Claire, by complicity—
were the evilest people I've ever known. Were, are. (I didn't
even think of ourselves then, when it happened, as *children*; I
didn't make that prime mistake of presuming we were innocent.
A child is an adult without any softening social graces—but
given an intensity of character which the years seem to take
away from you. That intensity can be terrifying. At the time
those two filled my perspective as fully as any grown-up did.)

Our families lived in a small Wiltshire town with an abbey,

famous for its picture-postcard looks. Alan's father was a senior
partner in a law firm, and did court work in Winchester; he was
well known for the sharpness of his brain and won all his cases
(even, it was said, when he had the proof his client was guilty).
His wife was his only failure to date. She'd done an unheard-of
thing: she'd run away. I heard my mother and her friends
discussing her, exchanging the rumours—someone thought
they'd seen her (or her double) attending in Harrods'
haberdashery; and because they knew her mother lived in
Hove, another time they decided she'd fled to Brighton for a
gad-fly life and she'd already been disgraced in some unmen-
tionable way. Claire's father was the second-in-charge at the
abbey, and decency personified; her roly-poly French mother
feelingly played Debussy on the piano at amateur concerts
fund-raising for the roof. My father was a doctor; my mother
was a scion of ancient, inbred blue-blood stock, she raised me
(rather tiredly) and belonged (indifferently) to the West of
England League of Lily-Growers and had afternoon bridge
sessions in the house when she could summon the energy to spin
the dial on the phone to muster her friends. This only matters
set against the truth of our three characters, what our lives had
made us: Alan—pushy and masterful like his father in the
courtroom, impatient, unscrupulous, unforgiving; Claire—
sensitive and thoughtful and conciliating like her decent father,
but in the end fickle and weak; and me—I don't know what,
nothing very much, careful, hesitant, testing, uncommitted,
and at the mercy of them both.

We were supposed to become friends simply because we lived in
genteel houses on the same pretty street. But the houses dated
back centuries and were built like little palazzi, fortresses with
high honeystone walls and railings and gates and hedges, and for
all we normally saw of other people's existences we could have
been living fields apart from them. There was also such a thing
as a residents' association recently got together to keep Foss

Street pretty and in the "right hands" and to judge on the colours of front doors and really our intended "friendship" so-called was just a consequence of that inspired gesture of adult self-interest.

My mother invited Alan to our house one day, a few months after his own mother's flight. She prodded me in the shoulder when she introduced us so I'd take him outside into the garden. (It meant I was to be "nice" to him.) Claire, who was my friend already, looked as embarrassed as I was feeling myself. The three of us played Grandma's Footsteps—"What's the time, Mr Wolf?"—but Alan was rather rough about it and had great delight catching us both. Claire and I had to sit down by the little pond for a breather.

It was Alan, standing over us watching us, who suggested it—out of the blue. "We'll build a tree house!" Claire said she'd never heard of a "tree house". I'd seen a photograph of the bush hotel on stilts where the Queen stayed in Kenya on her honeymoon and I thought of that. He decided the first fork on the old oak would be ideal. He ran back with us to ask my parents. They said "yes, of course", with kindly smiles for Alan's motherless condition.

It took a few days to build. It also gave Alan unlicensed access to my garden. At the weekend my father found us lengths of wood he hammered together to make a platform, with four more planks for a balustrade on each side. (Banging away, he told us there was a tradition of having bedrooms upstairs in houses because our ancestors, the cavemen, used to make *their* sleeping places in trees to be safe from predators. "Animals?" I asked him. "Yes. Or humans," he said.) Claire contributed some lopped branches from a pine tree in the vicarage garden: they still had their needles attached, and Alan without discussing it arranged them to make a chalet-style roof to give us shade. My father knotted some chandler's cable-rope to one of the other branches. Then it was more or less complete and ready. Claire's mother gave us two tins of condensed milk and a packet of

100

The Tree House

Playbox biscuits to fortify us. We thought the biscuits were a bit
juvenile: we were seven and would have appreciated digestives,
or ginger nuts, which are harder and you can nibble at longer.

We had the "opening" one afternoon when my parents were
out and the help didn't see me removing the soda syphon from
the sideboard. Claire squirted it at the trunk and said the proper
words, gleaned from abbey fête-openings. I followed Alan's
lead—but less earnestly—clapping and whistling. Then we each
shinned up the trunk. My shoulders strained with the
unaccustomed exercise. When we were up the three of us sat
down, but awkwardly. There was something not quite right. It
wasn't just the seasick feeling: maybe it was because the
planning and anticipation were over and we realized this was
what it had been in aid of and we didn't know how to begin.
Claire smiled sweetly at us, how her mother smiled on her
charity musical evenings. I smiled too—in the vague way my
mother did when she welcomed her professional bridge friends
to the house. Alan didn't smile. (Was it because he'd forgotten
how *his* mother used to smile, I wondered—if she ever had?) He
just watched us; he wouldn't stop looking at us, his eyes flicked
between us. Claire had phoned me up about the pine branches
in her garden without letting him know, and I thought he must
have taken it as a slight. Much more than that, I can see now—
it had been read as a deliberate cut, a prearranged snub, an
insult, a scornful challenge to his kingship. That was Alan. He
could always imagine things were any number of times worse
than they really were. Sitting there cross-legged his anger
seemed to be consuming him. I was fixed by the pull of his eyes.
From her to me, me to her, her to me, me to her. (Was it a habit
he'd picked up from his unhappy parents, when he sat witness
to the public-room silences like adjournments between their
prosecution bouts upstairs we used to hear with our windows
open, which my mother called their "blow-outs"? You couldn't
be sorry for him, though: Alan wasn't like that. I knew that even
my expertly diplomatic parents could only spare him their

101

tender smiles, not their sympathy. Already at seven he was ringed with barbed wire; his eyes hooked into you, tore flesh.) I think that for something so very little—Claire telling me first about the axed branches instead of him—he hated me.

I don't use the word lightly. My mother always forbade me to say it. "You dislike something strongly. . . ." she told me. I'm not sure what the difference was: maybe it sounded more elegant and less raw, put that way. But Alan didn't just "dislike strongly". Hating is a trait of paranoia, it fixes on the object, it belongs to an obsessive nature. His mother's days—until she abandoned husband and son—had been spent keeping the house as antiseptically dustless as a space capsule: in the evenings she would have to lie down in the bedroom with a migraine and that's when the famous quarrels began. That's how it began with Alan too, the inherited oddness, and then his father telling him (when she could hear) that his mother was off-the-beam.

The anger happened again about something else. I was used to the talk of my mother and her friends about that mania for cleanliness and order driving Alan's father to a frenzy—so now their home without anyone to look after them was reputed to be a midden of unmade beds and unwashed dishes. After several visits to the tree house, Claire started in like vein. She announced in a lecturing voice that we ought to have a "system" about things: for instance we should scrape the mud off our sandals before we climbed off the rope. She insisted the biscuits should be kept *there* and the top must always be kept tightly shut on the tin. Alan was hating it, his eyes flared at her. I took her side, by instinct I suppose, and said we needed "discipline". He told me very quietly—but spitting the words at me—to "sod off". He must have heard his father use the expression to his mother. It was new to Claire and me, although it sounded angry and we could guess its rudeness from the tone. I was feeling that incidents like this could only make the two of us closer, Claire and me (even when we weren't *meaning* to hurt him). Alan was smart enough to spot the complicity starting for himself. Claire—patching up—asked him to open one of our two precious tins of condensed milk with the tin opener. He saw through that ruse. "Ask *him*," he told her, his eyes tightening on me. "You can have one of your own," she said to placate him with a new energy and desperation in her voice. But he wasn't listening to her and got up and swung off down the rope. (He was easily the best at that. He'd seen a Tarzan film on television. Neither of us—see how I make the association?—neither Claire nor I in our separate homes were allowed to watch television as indiscriminately as he did.)

"Anyway," I shouted after him, stuck for anything else to say, "it's *my* garden." It sounded crass and stupid and the words seemed to float in the air without going away. He walked over and started to jump up and down on the rope, drumming his fists on the boards of our floor. The house rocked, like a boat on waves. Claire screamed and clutched my arm. "Please, please tell him to stop!" I didn't want to tell him any such thing. He kept thumping his fists on the planks. "Oh, make him stop!" I didn't know what to do. I couldn't let him get away with the outrage, but I realized things were just about over between us and I wanted it to be all *his* doing, not mine. I was determined. (Can you be determined at seven? Why not, as at twenty-seven or seventy-seven?) The raft of planks we were standing on began to tilt. The blows shuddered up through my legs. Claire was in tears, waving at him. "Please stop, please stop! *Alan!*"

And it stopped. That was all he was wanting her to do—say his name. I shut my eyes, opened them again: I'd thought I was going to be sick with the motion. In a moment he was perfectly gentle and he was helping her to slide down the rope. She was shaking and had to lean on him. I blinked at the two of them walking off together through the haze of summer insects.

Another afternoon there was a domestic mix-up: I was supposed to be going to Salisbury with my parents after lunch, but something happened and we stayed at home. I climbed up into the tree house, which my father had made safe again, and called at the top of my voice over the orchard into Claire's parents' walled garden. She was outside and heard me and did a Red Indian whoop. "Tell Alan!" I cried to her. Claire whooped and shouted "Alan!" in the other direction, but her voice wouldn't have been strong enough to carry that extra distance. I think I knew that when I asked her. I'd never tried these jungle calls before (the information came from Alan, watching Johnny Weissmuller on television). But I understood straightaway what the significance of this novel method of communication was, that the weakness of Claire's voice gave me an excellent means of excluding Alan any time I didn't want him.

So Claire came on her own and we had a pleasant afternoon up in the tree, out of sight of the house. We chatted and compared our shadows slowly lengthening on the grass towards the pond. We lay on our backs and listened to the lazy hum of insects under us. We must have started to doze because we were invaded before we seemed to understand what was happening. One moment tranquillity and contentment with our day, the next Alan flying off the end of the rope and the tree house was an echo-box. "A-*ha*!" He stamped a war dance with his bare feet, laughing at the shock on our faces. He was dressed up like a crazy pirate. He had red stuff like lipstick smeared on his cheeks and a curtain ring over one ear and a bright yellow towel for a cummerbund. "Well, well, well!" It sounded just like his father talking to his mother, when his voice used to travel to us on a still night and before she packed her bags and ran away. He pushed on my chest with his foot so I couldn't get up. "Well, well, *well*!" He kept saying it, smiling down into my face. But none of this was meant to be fun.

He bent over me and dragged me across the platform by my arms. I tried scraping my heels on the floor like brakes then twisting my bottom from side to side to slow him, but nothing could have succeeded against his strength and purpose. My head was suddenly hanging over the edge with empty space underneath. "Well, well, *well*!" He wasn't laughing any more. Claire called to him to stop. He told her "Shut your mouth!" Then I seemed to be back inside again, on all-fours, and he was booting me in the bottom chanting, "Out! Out! Out!" Claire had her hands on his shoulders. "Please don't, Alan! Please don't!" He flung the rope at me: I held on but I was shaking like jelly and when I slithered down it went burning through my palms. I fell on my back on the grass and the pain made me start to cry. Alan had landed behind me and was yelling at Claire to come down. He grabbed my arm and began to pull me like a dead body. I saw where he was making for, the pond. "Go on, take his legs!" Claire came running after us. "What are you going to do?" "Take his legs! Do as I say or I'll throw you in too!" I don't suppose she felt she had any choice and she tried to lift my weight; she couldn't and dropped my legs and then picked them up again when Alan said he would twist her arm. He called her a "bloody woman" and she burst into tears at such foulness. She let me go and Alan pulled me the rest of the way, quicker so he didn't lose his resolve. I believe that at seven he had the badness in him to know I would be his revenge on the world.

As I tried scrambling up off the flagstones, hands pushed into my aching back which sent me pitching forwards again. I could hear screams and shouts from my mother and her bridge friends who'd seen. I crashed into the water and the cold was like splitting ice. My eyes opened and I seemed to be tumbling through space, passing stars. My arms must have floated up and the rest of me too, for after the blackness I was on my back seeing a blue summer sky shining absurdly far away from me. The branches of the tree were like cracks in a blue plate. Then between me and them I saw two faces peering down, the crazy pirate's, and the one behind with a wondering look. Out of the sky two arms came reaching into the water, but not (as I thought it must be) to save me. They seemed to want to hold me down, not help me up. The striped face dropped closer, and at one point I was making the connection, that the arms belonged to *him*. Alan. His white hands fluttered above me like sea anemones in a swell. I felt them fastening on my neck and I tried in the coldness to find them with my own hands. I locked them on something but I didn't know any more if it was him or me. I'd gone down and bobbed up again and my head must have made a hole in the water because I could hear the panic of high voices. I think I went down again—or twice more—before there was an explosion of water and through it other arms were reaching in to rescue me. I felt a different kind of strength in them, and I gave myself willingly.

They lay me on the grass and it was what I saw when I could open my eyes to observe the world—the tree house—above their heads, beyond their concern, where the clouds seemed to have torn to fleece on the oak's branches. It was riding the afternoon very precariously. A sudden wind might bring it down. My mother saw me looking. "Daddy'll repair it," she said through tears and she tried to make me more comfortable till he came, brushing off insects with her scented handkerchief.

If he does repair it, I was thinking, I live in it alone this time. I saw afternoons ahead, and books, and biscuits, and watching into people's rooms and never being seen. For a moment, with the sun finding me through the grid of branches and warming my face, I seemed to be picking wisdom ripe out of that blue air.

Rachel Gould

A PRIVATE VIEW
MRS ELIZABETH DAVIES
THUCYDIDES

A Private View

You may have seen the item about my brother's disappearance in the newspaper. Not the national newspapers, of course—the local newspaper, the *Oxford Times*. It was only a small item, in the section entitled "Waifs and strays", by which they mean bits of unexplained news: the bag of strangled babies someone fished out of the Thames at Abingdon, the labourer found with his throat cut in Summertown. The sort of news you read quickly, or skip over, because they are just bare facts that have no connection with anything that you know about.

"A Puzzling Disappearance", it said. "Mr Paul Roberts, second son of Professor and Mrs Roberts of Compas, Iffley Road, has disappeared in the strangest of circumstances. Mr Roberts had rooms in Christ Church and was due to commence his Classical Moderation examination yesterday. He did not appear at the schools. On enquiry at Compas on Tuesday, it was stated that Mr Roberts had been studying over-hard for his examination, and may have been over-wrought. The family has not so far heard of his whereabouts."

That was more than two weeks ago, and no one has heard from him since. Mother told me that the newspaper-man had been again to make more enquiries, but that she had refused to speak with him. Mother is pretending not to worry, but in fact she worries very much. The newspaper-man thinks that she knows more than she will say, but my parents know nothing. The others know nothing either. Only I have, perhaps, a small clue. But if it means what I think it means, I cannot tell anyone. I cannot prove what I suspect, and if I could it would be immensely difficult to explain, and they would try to avoid the implications, and simply say that Alice is being fanciful again.

I suppose they would be afraid of a scandal. It is some time now since the Wilde case, and I remember hearing Paul say that everyone, now, thinks quite differently, that ideas on that subject are more liberal. Of course, it is difficult for me to tell, as I don't see very many people, but I have my doubts. One thing that I can say with certainty is that my parents' ideas are emphatically not liberal. They might rather never hear from Paul again, than discover . . . I am no nearer understanding how my parents can be happy within the confines of their narrow morality than I was when I first started thinking about it. Other people who go to church seem able to listen attentively to the sermon, speak politely to the vicar when they leave, and pass their week without giving these problems further thought. But my parents are trapped by their acute and ever-present sense of sin. My mother tortures herself with guilt over the slightest cross word she speaks to any of us. There seems to be no spontaneity in either of them: they watch themselves constantly for any falling away. Original sin is real for them. They have never understood Paul because he is so different. Or so I thought.

I shall try to explain what happened. But it will be in a circuitous fashion, because that is the only explanation. I mean, I feel that his disappearance is partly my fault; that, if I had understood him completely, he would have had an ally. Oh! we have been *so* close, and yet I didn't see—it is such a terrible admission to have to make. All I have to do is to think, and I prided myself on my sensitivity, on the depth of my comprehension. Yet I have failed him in the one thing where I could, and should, have been of some help—and so, in a sense, I have failed him completely. There was only me who could have helped. None of the others can take a hint without having their ankles kicked hard, as it were, at the same time. Cedric is bound up in his career—he is a doctor up in London; William is

110

also heavily involved in his own life—he is still at home, but since he has discovered that not all women are as feeble and sickly as I, we have hardly seen him; and Terence, although he is adorable, as everyone agrees, is still too young for the sort of talking that Paul needed. That leaves me. Of course, we are the closest in age too. There is only a little over a year between us. But that isn't it.

You see, I am the only girl in the family. Paul, for me, has been not only a brother, but the sister I have always so much wanted. He makes no distinction between girls' things and boys' things: our conversation can take in everything. There are no boundaries. When he comes to sit by my bed, we can talk for hours. There is never time enough for all we have to say to each other. And, if I were too tired for politics, or to hear about his college friends, he would read to me. That is one thing we have in common that sets us apart from the others. We have read everything that has come out recently: all of Hardy, and Arnold, who is an especial favourite of Paul's, Ruskin, Gide even. When Paul went to France last year, he brought me back Gide's most recent book—in French. It gave me great pleasure, a very dubious pleasure, no doubt, to know that all my slaving over that language had been of some use. One should not be proud of one's accomplishments, I know—Mother is always telling me so—but now that so many of my others are of no use to me, I keep my French going as best I can. Of what use is it to be able to play the piano if you are never well enough to get up and play? Books are like friends for me. I am so lonely, and they are my best company. I don't feel that I am making unreasonable demands of them to be with me all the time. Paul is the only one who does not make me feel that he visits me as a duty; he seems not to notice the medicine bottles lined up on the mantelpiece, or the warm fug that builds up sometimes because Mother is so afraid for me to have the window open. On the rare occasions when William comes up to sit with me, I am always half sure that it is because Mother has sent him. He won't sit in the little chair by my bed, keeps going to the window to look at the garden, cannot think of anything to say. We just make one another nervous.

I *know* it is a long time to be ill. I *know* how much William hates illness, and thinks of it as a weakness, as though I were ill by a failure of will on my part. But every time I have felt better, and have gone downstairs, I have always had an attack, and now Mother won't hear of my leaving my room. I wish, I wish I would be better! Do they think I want never to do anything, never to be anything but an invalid, dependent on others? Of course, I can't tell them, or not as I feel it; I have to be grateful, because *they* are looking after me, I depend on *them*. It was bad enough to be the only girl in the family, to be always demure, to have to sew while they were all learning Latin and Greek, to know that I would always be stupid while they were going to be educated to such a pitch of fine consciousness. And now, almost two years of being an invalid and no sign of my getting really better. How will I survive?

You might think it a nice life, never having to do anything. You? You don't exist, of course. I've invented you to take an interest in me, as there is no one real. You are the person I want to understand, who will listen, question me, really try to find out. Simply being a woman they take less interest in you. You do not work, you have no powerful friends that people want to hear about as they sit round the table for dinner; you don't do anything except sew, play the piano, read French. And if you are a woman who is ill, you recede further into the background. They call it invalidism, but it might as well be called invalidity. I had such ambitions. Paul was going to find out for me about the new college for women, where Miss Wordsworth is principal. I would have worked and worked to get there. She would never have had a more brilliant pupil than I would have been.

You see, I am not lazy. Even now, I am trying to know as much as possible. I read, I listen to what my visitors tell me, I think about it, put two and two together, make connections, come to conclusions. I am sure that some people would be astonished at what a girl of twenty who is bed-ridden and who never goes out into the world *can* know. And that was where Paul has been such a help. He is my eyes, my detective almost. He goes out and looks at things for me, very hard, at all the details—what people are wearing, what they said, whether they are fat or thin or have swollen red hands or smooth white ones, how they trim their hats, which flowers have opened in the Parks this week, whether the deer have foaled yet in Magdalen. And then he comes back and tells me, so beautifully I can see everything myself. He always liked to tell things, stories, or just what something looked like—the sky in a storm or a picture he had been to see at the Ashmolean, and now for me he does it better and better. I should say, did. Perhaps he never will again. There, I'm telling you all about myself, but I have not told you what happened.

It was the week before last. Paul was coming home for dinner. This was just before his examination, and he had been working very hard and had not been to see me as often as he usually did. I heard him arrive—my room is above the roof of the porch where the pebble drive comes down the side of the house, and I know everybody's footsteps now. He came up briefly before dinner, and promised to come back afterwards for a proper talk. I thought he looked strained, and thinner. I ate my own small supper very quickly—Mary brought it up on a tray —and then I waited impatiently for Paul to come. I could hear the dinner going on—it lasted a long time, because my parents had invited the President of Corpus and his wife, and that delightful old man, Mr Dodgson, who teaches Mathematics at Paul's college. There was a steady murmur of conversation: the door that opens from the dining room into the hall must have been left slightly open; the clink of silver on Mother's best plates; and finally the scraping of chairs as Mother and Mrs Chase got up to leave the men for brandy or port. Then Mr Chase's voice dominated the others' in the dining room—he is a terrible bore, I always think. Paul told me once that he is famous among undergraduates for the letter he wrote to *The Times* when the idea of a women's college in the University was first debated, saying that real solid learning would now be replaced by "the art of conversation at tea parties". His wife is the sort of soft, self-sacrificing woman you would expect a man like that to have. I mean, she is very nice, and plays the piano with impeccable technique and no feeling whatsoever, and speaks perfect French.

At last Paul came up. He did not climb over the banisters at the head of the stairs as he often used to do when he knew that Mother would not see him, but came round the landing, slowly, to my room, which is at the very end.

"Enfin," I said. "What can you possibly have found to talk about for all that time? I thought you might go without coming to see me."

"It's true, I can't stay for very long. I have to get back and work a little before I go to bed."

He sat down on the little chair, the one with the cushions that Mother embroidered when she was very young. There was a swatch of stuffs on my bed, some William Morris ones that Mother had brought back from Liberty's on her most recent visit to town, thinking that I might be cheered by some new drapes in the latest fashion. He picked them up and fingered them absent-mindedly for a little, looking round the room. I realize now that he was trying to fix it in his mind, knowing that he might not see it again for a long time. I watched him, admiring his clothes—he was wearing a new suit which fitted him admirably, with a strange Oriental-looking tie-pin stuck in his green cravat. He always had dressed exquisitely from the time, very early on, when he had started taking an interest in clothes. He was not a fop, but he had a fine, almost feminine, taste for the colours that went together most subtly. Perhaps that was a clue that I should have noticed earlier.

"These are nice," he said. "Have you chosen one?"

"I wanted to ask your advice about them. Do you like the bluey one best, or the one with the reds and oranges? I really can't decide. Mother says the red is too bright and will aggravate my nerves, but I think it is so beautiful, that perhaps it will make me feel more alive."

He looked at them again, but didn't answer. He did not seem to want to talk at all, but I had not waited all that impatient time to sit with him in silence, however amicable.

"What have you been doing?" I asked.

"Oh, you know, working. I've been working solidly for the last month. But somehow, now, I've lost my enthusiasm. I wake early almost every day, frightened, leap out of bed to my desk, and then somehow I find myself just sitting, for hours, with nothing done. Staring out of the window, you know, into the quad, watching people go past. Perhaps I've been working too hard. That's what Mother says, but I do so want to do well that I can't relax for a moment. On Monday though . . . on Monday I went on the river with Robert. Do you remember me telling you about Robert? I can't remember if I've mentioned him to you."

"Of course you have. The one with the sister who has just come up to Somerville."

"You do have a marvellous memory. He . . . we have become great friends recently. You have no idea what a relief it has been to find someone who thinks like me—on nearly every subject, you know, we have the same ideas, the same feelings, ambitions. He's not one of the usual hearty, fox-hunting types. . . ."

"What about me though? What about me? Don't I think the same, don't I come up to your level?"

"Oh, yes. Yes, of course. But, I mean, in college. He's the first one, the first I've found. To talk about books, you know, like we do, and read poetry, stay up half the night thinking and talking. The only one who gives me a strong sense of being myself, of it being right to be someone like me."

"But how can you ever doubt it? Being so brilliant, and so handsome, and above all, so nice." I said it in a jocular tone, but

115

I meant it very seriously.

"Nice? I'm not so sure that I am that nice."

"Well, I'm sure, if you're not. How would I survive if you didn't come and see me?"

"Oh, of course you would. With the others, and Mother who never tires of looking after you."

"Yes, but the others don't really *know*. It's you who are most important to me."

"Well, you are important to me too. I wish you could meet Robert, you know," he said, inconsequentially. "He's so like us. It wasn't a complete holiday, Monday, on the river. We took Plato with us, and I read to Robert while he punted, and then we changed places and he read while I took my turn. And then we discussed it. It's the Symposium I really love. The part about the two halves desperately searching for one another to make a whole. Robert and I . . . "

"What?"

"Oh, nothing. Something rather silly I was going to say." He paused. "It's such a pity that we could never persuade Father to teach you the classics. There are some wonderful things in them."

"I wish *you* would teach me. Perhaps when you have finished your degree you might have time." I looked at him, I suppose adoringly—I always found it difficult to disguise how strongly I felt about him. Normally, he would hold my eyes, and we would have a slow secret smile together in thanksgiving that we had each other. But this evening he seemed to find my looks embarrassing, as though such strong affection as mine demanded more of him than he thought he could give. He blushed slightly, and seemed to be on the verge of saying something, something difficult, which needed to be said in a careful way, choosing the right words. He had an air of thinking intently, not really about what I was saying, but about something that was preoccupying him, and that had been all evening. Then suddenly, from the drawing room, the clear sound of the piano rose up the stairwell. It was not Mother playing. Her repertoire, although she played well, was small, and consisted mostly of Mozart, with a few of the easier Beethoven sonatas and some Bach. This was a piece I had never heard before: very elegant, light, vague I would have said, and yet with an atmosphere of rather terrible sadness. It was executed well, and with feeling, so that, as I knew it must be Mrs Chase playing, I began to wonder if my impression of her as a woman in whom every flicker of emotion was suppressed might not be premature. But perhaps anyone who played that particular piece would have sounded like some sad poet pouring out a dreadful love affair to whomever would listen sympathetically. I turned to glance quickly at Paul, and saw that he was listening in rapt attention. We listened in silence, but not together, so it seemed to me. The music drew Paul out of my presence. I was with his ghost, just the outer semblance of his body. All his thoughts had travelled away from this room, to somewhere else altogether, where I could not follow him. I felt an unutterable loneliness.

The piece was not long, and as the last chords sang through the big house, Paul looked up. "I suppose that proves", he said, "that there are some people still today who really think about things, who really feel. Not just going for the outside of things only, I mean—seeing the whole lot, right down deep, and prepared to express what they see there."

I suppose I agreed with him—I usually did—but this music had made me jealous, and I hoped that Mrs Chase would not be prevailed upon to play again. So I sighed with relief when I heard the Chases and Mr Dodgson leaving, Mr Chase making a speech of thanks at the front door—so long that he must have composed it before the evening began. Their feet scrunched along the drive and we heard Mr Chase hail a cab.

But in fact their leaving was unlucky. Immediately they had gone, Mother sent Mary up to tell Paul that he really mustn't tire me any longer, and to ask him to come in and say goodnight to her before he left. He stood up, slowly, as though he did not really want to go just yet, and went over to the small window, looking out across the porch and the lawn with its long flower-beds of roses and lupins to the copper beech at the garden-end and the college playing-fields beyond that.

"You ought to ask Mother to have some roses cut for you before they finish," he said after a time. And then, in a rush, "Why do you think, Alice, that women are always more gentle than men? I had such a horrid experience on Monday. We were coming back in the punt to Folly Bridge, and just as we got to the barges there was a whole boatload of Christ Church men swinging into the Isis. So we had to pass them very close, and Robert was punting, and we grazed the side of their boat, and they jeered, all of them, and Robert blushed furiously."

"Why? Why did they jeer at you?"

"Oh, they loathe us. Particularly since we have become such friends."

"But why?"

"I don't really know. They think we're indecently serious about learning. They probably saw the Plato. They try and appear even more brutish than they really are. And I suppose we dress rather too flamboyantly for their taste. Taste!" he repeated, disgustedly. "They don't have any really. Not one iota. There they were, red-faced to a man, and God knows how many bottles, all empty, they were trailing along on a piece of string behind the boat."

He made them sound the picture of ridiculousness, and I laughed.

"You wouldn't have thought they were funny if you could have seen them yourself."

"You shouldn't mind if they don't like you."

"No, I know. But why did they have to make Robert so shamefaced?"

"Well, he shouldn't mind either."

"No. No, but you see, he just does. He's made like that. And since Monday he's hardly spoken to me, they made him so conscious."

"Conscious? Conscious of what?"

"Well, of himself. Of our friendship, and of what might strike others as strange about it."

"But if you say these others are such Philistines, why should it bother you? If they don't understand, why should you care? They don't sound worth any worry. . . . "

"Yes, but it isn't that only. It's . . . it's something else. . . . "

I had been concentrating hard on what he was saying, and only then did we hear Mother's footsteps, half-way round the landing. Then she was at the door.

"Paul, my dear, don't you think you ought to go? Didn't Mary come up a moment ago with my message? I really think poor Alice will be tired by any longer conversation."

"Yes. I'm sorry, Mother. You know how we are, we start talking, and then we just forget what the time is."

"I know, but isn't it rather selfish of you? Alice will feel horribly languid tomorrow, and not like doing anything at all."

"But I don't do anything anyway, Mother."

"Oh, Alice! You've got on quite far with your sampler, and I wanted to ask you tomorrow if you wouldn't write for me to Cedric. I shall be so busy with the arrangements for the garden party, and you know how Cedric relies on me not to miss a week."

Paul and I exchanged a small commiserating glance, and then he bent to kiss me. I thought his kiss was warmer than usual, and assumed that it was in compensation for the task that Mother had set me. Of all of us, Cedric is the most practical and literal-minded, and to write a letter to him with any literary merit whatsoever is a difficult venture.

"And now, Alice, I will give you your medicines, and then you must turn down the lamp and go to sleep quickly."

Mother always makes me feel like a small child.

"Goodnight, Alice," said Paul, and made me a little mock

119

bow as he went out of the door, in a manner which was more characteristic of him than the rather morose conversation we had had that evening.

So that was what happened. You might think there was nothing in it to make me understand his disappearance, and if I told Mother what we had talked about, she would make nothing of it either. But then, she never took the pressures he was under very seriously. Or even, perhaps, he never told her what he felt. You know that it is easy to give the bare bones of facts about what you do, how you spend your day; but to express the feelings that underlie those facts and days is much more difficult. I think that Paul was trying to tell me, without saying it in so many words, that his friendship with Robert was more than an ordinary friendship. But he did not feel he could tell me that straight out, and I was being so selfish and egotistical that I did not realize he was trying to make me understand something out of the ordinary.

I think some fear of scandal has made Paul go away. And if he has gone away, I think I know where he will have gone—to Paris. Paul loved Paris. I only know the city through him, of course, but the way he described it made it seem a wonderful place. The sunshine, the balconies, the window-boxes of red geraniums, the parks and the boulevards and the cafés. And above all, the people, he said—so elegantly dressed, and so cultured, as though they had imbibed a different sensibility from the English sort with their *café au lait* every morning. So I think he will have gone there.

You think, perhaps, that I should be upset about this friendship between my brother and Robert? But how can I be when that stems from his whole character? I would not want him to change and be like the others. He is delightful and charming and a little odd, but his oddness is his particular charm. Father is horrified that he has not sat his examination, and Mother is distraught that he should go away without telling her, but I—I am simply waiting. He must write soon, and then, if he gives an address, I shall write back and tell him everything I have thought. He must come back. He is the only one who thinks of me as a real person.

Mrs Elizabeth Davies

At the beginning of his career, no one knew that Miles Davies had a wife. No one, that is, who counted. He did not count their neighbours, or the few friends they had kept from college days, who did of course know that he had a wife, and who tended to treat the Davies, as people generally do treat couples, as a corporate personality, not as two individuals who happen to be married.

These people did not count. The people who counted for Miles Davies were the magazine editors and programme producers who bought what he wrote, and helped him in his career. These people were largely unaware that he was married. Perhaps they noticed that the same woman's voice answered the telephone when they wanted to speak to Miles about numbers of words and rearranged deadlines, but they probably thought that this soft, well-mannered voice belonged to a secretary. Of course, writers do need secretaries—especially writers whose careers are taking off, as Miles's was—and in fact Elizabeth was in a sense his secretary. She dealt with what Miles thought of as the uncreative side of being a writer. She made fair copies of his work, answered requests for interviews, corrected his proofs, and protected him from the people he didn't want to have to do with.

People think, Miles would say, that a writer's life is easy, but of course there is as much drudgery for a writer as for a factory worker on an assembly line. The person he was talking to would nod sympathetically over the difficulties of a writer's life. It was an idea he often brought out for interviewers, and often the interviewers themselves were aspiring to be writers (this was why they found Miles Davies so fascinating, because he always had a great deal to say about the writer's vocation, about the terrible tensions of creativity and the fertile wells of the subconscious), and so they were well aware of the drudgery that must be involved in hammering out an idea and rounding off its corners. Mostly the interviewers finished their interviews without finding out that an Elizabeth Davies had anything to do with the perfectly finished poems and experimental prose that appeared so regularly now in establishment and avant-garde magazines. On a very few occasions, Elizabeth might bring a tray of blue Chinese bowls, a pot of jasmine tea with flowers floating in it, and a plate of finely-sliced lemon pieces into the book-lined study while an interview was going on. The interviewer would notice that she was rather beautiful—but you expected the wife of Miles Davies to be beautiful—and would jot down a note about pale flowers floating in exquisitely clear tea and, when she had gone, would ask Miles, "Is that your wife?"

"Yes," he would say.

"What does she do?"

"Elizabeth? Well, I suppose you would call her a housewife."

So, if Elizabeth ever appeared in any of the articles about Miles, she appeared as a housewife. The readers understood the rest without prodding: Miles had married her when he was very young, simply because she was beautiful; but she was obviously an empty face without ideas, without creative genius except in the matter of making a tea-tray look like a Braque still life. They realized that Miles must repent having married such a woman before he had met the brilliant, intellectual women he must meet as he grew increasingly famous.

In fact, Miles Davies had met Elizabeth at Oxford. He had been studying English, and so had she. If he had got a first-class degree and she a second, there were some among their friends who were unkind enough to think that this was rather because of his facility in picking up the vocabulary of avant-garde critics, than because he was intrinsically more intelligent than she was. Miles was a brilliant talker, and for most people that was enough to signal a brilliant mind. She was more reticent, and took time to be convinced that people were worth talking to. Sometimes this made her appear arrogant and anti-social to new acquaintances, but, on the other hand, a friend once made was kept for a long time. Miles always had new, very good friends, wonderful people when he first met them, generally somewhat less wonderful when he had known them for a few weeks, who drifted away to be replaced by other wonderful people. In a sense, Elizabeth was his only real friend.

In his public life, as it became wider in scope, she organized and protected him; in their private life she also protected him, though he was unaware of it. She had discovered early in their relationship that he hated competition, especially among people who were close to him, and she had begun, almost unconsciously, to avoid giving him the impression that she competed with him in any field. She knew, although he never said so, that he had been relieved when she did not get a first class degree as she had been expected to do: their relative intellectual standing was thus irrefutably established. And she knew also that he did not take her literary ambitions very seriously. When they had met, he had been glad to discover that she *had* literary ambitions—it meant he could talk to her about the dreadful solitude of the writer, and know she would understand. He also liked to talk to her about poetry: she had a good mind, and her comments often supplied an emotional reaction which he lacked. But when she wanted to talk to him about his own writing, he became vague and uncommunicative.

"I can't tell you," he would say, as though saddened by the immutable ways of the literary mind. "If I do, it'll all be dissipated, all be divided into little bits and never come together again, however hard I think about it. You know, if you talk about things, they disappear—they're replaced by what you said about them. If I could explain everything to you, I wouldn't need to write poetry at all."

Then he might kiss her, as a consolation for all the things he couldn't say to her, but these were kisses she never liked very much. They were too like the sweets you give to a child to make up for not having time to take it to the zoo. They had married before the end of the last college year, and as soon as they moved to London, to a small flat near Regent's Park, their days assumed a fixed rhythm, which Miles affected to despise, but which was essential to his work. Elizabeth got up first and made him a cup of tea which he drank in bed while she had a bath and made breakfast. They ate together, at the green-baize card table covered with a starched white cloth, which stood next to the only window in the flat with a view over the park. This was Elizabeth's favourite time of the day. Miles was still relaxed and hadn't begun on the curve of mounting tension which often resulted from his being unable to write as much or as well as he wanted. Miles got dressed and went to his study where he remained all day, incommunicado except for the most important telephone calls. He said that if he broke off for lunch he lost his thread; she made sandwiches and left them in the kitchen for him to collect when he was hungry.

During the first few months of their marriage, he made a point of asking her about what she had done during the day, but after a time he forgot to do this, and so he was never fully aware that she was writing, too. Elizabeth herself thought of her writing as amateur. He was the professional, the well-known writer, the one who made the money. She was afraid to show him what she wrote, partly because she was afraid it wasn't good and partly because he might think she was trying to compete with him. He was used to the sound of her typing in another room; he knew she did other things apart from making good copies of his own work, but he wasn't sufficiently interested to ask what those things were. After a time she had several stories finished and retyped, and without mentioning to Miles what she was doing, she sent them off to various magazines with stamped addressed envelopes, and waited to see what would happen. Several weeks elapsed, and two of the stories had been returned with impersonal notes of rejection, when she received a letter from an editor:

Dear Mrs Davies

Thank you for sending us your story *The Hospital Visit*. The Fiction Editor and I have both read it with a great deal of pleasure. I particularly liked the tense scene between the ward sister and the mother of the child: it shows great understanding of very complex emotions. There are a few changes which we hope you will agree to make, but we are interested in using the story, possibly in one of the autumn issues. Our general terms are £50 per 1,000 words. I hope you will agree to this.

We are always looking for new writers of talent, and would be pleased to see any other stories you may have to show us. Will you arrange an appointment with Miss Keyes, the Fiction Editor, so that she can explain the changes we would like made?

Yours sincerely . . .

The post did not arrive until Miles had already withdrawn to his study, but Elizabeth was so elated by her success that she seriously considered interrupting him with the news. After a few minutes of contemplating the letter, though, she realized she could not, and waited in agitation until he should come out to get his sandwiches from the kitchen. She tried to absorb herself in housework, but those couple of hours passed with dreadful slowness. From time to time she heard bursts of staccato hammerings from his typewriter, interspersed with pauses which got progressively longer as the morning advanced. The chair in front of his desk creaked as he got up repeatedly and sat down again, and she knew from the brittle tapping of a pencil on glass that he was standing looking out of the window into the street below, searching among the parked cars and small running children for some inspired words.

At one o'clock exactly the door opened abruptly and Miles appeared scowling. Seeing her, he leant against the door jamb, drumming his fingertips silently in his palms, a characteristic gesture. "This damn thing won't come," he said after looking at her for a few seconds in a strange way. She waited for him to say more, but he lurched suddenly with his shoulder against the door and disappeared into the kitchen where she heard him fill the kettle and make himself coffee. He didn't think to offer her any. It didn't seem a good time to show him her triumph. He passed her chair in silence carrying the plate of sandwiches and mug of coffee, shutting the study door behind him—not loudly, but definitely. Elizabeth thought she would tell him in the evening.

An afternoon in the flat in her state of excitement was unthinkable, and she had a strong feeling of wanting to do something exotic, something she hadn't done for a long time. She picked up her bag and the flat keys and went down to the street. Perhaps Miles would again be looking out of the window, she thought, but didn't look up. Her heels clicked purposefully along the pavement. She went out with no definite idea in her mind, but a short walk along the edge of the park brought her to a café. She remembered now having noticed signs announcing that it would open shortly. Although it was still early in summer, the air was warm. Green-tinted sunshine filtered through the trees on the park edge on to several multicoloured umbrellas surmounting the café tables on the pavement. Elizabeth sat down at one of these. She wouldn't normally have exposed herself willingly to the danger of being stared at, but today she felt almost brash with confidence.

A waiter interrupted her absorbed reverie, sparked by the letter which she had with her in her bag. She ordered coffee, and a large piece of chocolate cake to make a private celebration. The afternoon was slow in wearing on, but she sat quite contentedly with a growing feeling of freedom at her unaccustomed independence. Miles had always considered that people were his province; they were for him to use and describe. But now that one of her own stories had been accepted, she saw that she could use them, too. The passers-by suddenly interested her more than they had ever done before. They were all potential stories, if only she could grasp them well enough. She noticed the odd ways in which they walked, caught scraps of conversation which suggested incidents and points of view far removed from her own life, noted the details of people's dress as they came and went through the gates of the park opposite. Finally, after the last pinstriped businessman had passed her on the way from the Tube station to his house up the hill, she got up and walked slowly home, her mind full of drifting images.

As she put the key in the door and pushed it quietly open she could almost smell the tension that had built up while she had been away. She went into the sitting room and opened both the windows as wide as they would go, as though the outside air would clear the fetid atmosphere inside. She was aware of Miles watching her do this, sunk in the armchair just outside his study door in an attitude of such wretched dejection that she would have been sympathetic if she had not been so conscious of her own happy buoyancy.

"Aren't you feeling well?" she asked, knowing perfectly well what the matter was, but trying to be tactful.

"I'm perfectly well, thank you, but my writing isn't. It's got one of those creeping diseases, that start off small but spread increasingly rapidly all over the place. This morning I was slow, but at least I got something done; this afternoon I've managed three sentences and they're lousy. All lousy."

"I'm sorry," Elizabeth said, meaning it, but unable to prevent herself from smiling at his metaphor. He noticed her smile as she turned away. It aggravated him.

"Where have you been all this time, anyway?"

"Just for a walk," she replied, trying to keep a sudden feeling of brusqueness out of her voice.

All evening she waited for Miles to escape from his debilitating mood, but he seemed to cling to it, tenaciously, as though he knew that she had something to tell him, and wanted to prevent it. At ten o'clock when they went to bed, she still hadn't told him. For some time after this, events and Miles's unapproachability conspired against her mentioning the story to him, and as his birthday was quite near, she decided simply to present him with a copy of the magazine on the morning of his birthday. At college, Miles had always celebrated his birthday in great style, as befits the *enfant terrible* and leading literary light of a year. There had been Buck's Fizz, cake from the Straw Hat in Summertown, and as many red candles regimented on the mantelpiece as the number of years he was celebrating. Two years in London had gone past without any real occasion, and Miles decided that his twenty-fifth birthday shouldn't suffer the same fate. Although it was not so much a cause for celebration, he joked, as for commiseration—he was now in his late twenties, and might just as well be middle aged. His girth had grown at the same rate at which his inspiration had dwindled so that now the only thing left for his friends to do with him was to bemoan the collapse of a great artistic talent under the forces of materialism. He said these things to his acquaintances on days when he was most full of himself and his increasing fame, and would have been surprised if anyone had agreed with him. But his wonderful friends vehemently protested his genius, and Miles smiled in a satisfied way at Elizabeth, who was the only one to have her doubts. Now that she had succeeded in having something of her own published, she was somehow not so impressed by Miles's genius. Her feelings about him were changing subtly.

The day of Miles's birthday began auspiciously. September had drawn out in an Indian summer that seemed never to want to prepare for the onset of bleaker weather. The trees on the park edge showed still virulently green from the sitting-room window, and the few sudden cloud bursts only contrasted pleasingly with the long hours of gentle sunshine. A faint grey mist hanging in the park had cleared by ten o'clock when Elizabeth, awake early, carried the breakfast tray into the bedroom.

"My God, champagne! *And* croissants. You're spoiling me, you wicked girl."

"Happy birthday, Miles," she said, handing him the cards that had arrived by the first post. "Do you know, I think even your father's remembered. There's one with a Horsham postmark."

"Can't have done. He hasn't since I went away to school. Makes him feel too old himself to think how old I must be now."

"Well, nothing would surprise me less. After all, you've become someone now. Perhaps he thinks you're worth knowing after all. But I hope he's not going to have one of his inspirations and turn up during the party."

"Oh, I don't know. I'll put him in a corner with a stiff gin and Frederica, and I'm sure he'll be quite happy. He'd be impressed by the people I can muster."

Elizabeth sat at the end of the bed, watching Miles open his cards one by one, waiting for him to have finished. She nervously fingered the brown paper package that she held behind her back.

"And this", she said, "is a little present from me. I'm giving you your real one this afternoon, but I wanted you to have this when no one else was here." She felt herself blushing after this short speech, but Miles didn't notice as he leant forward to take the package from her hand. He tore the brown paper unceremoniously and the shiny picture of a woman's head under an absurdly large hat appeared.

"What is it?"

"Well, you have to look. Look at the index and you'll see what it is."

He ran his eyes cursorily down the line of names, missed hers, and went back slowly to the top of the column.

130

Mrs Elizabeth Davies

"Page 80," she said. "Three and a half pages by me. It's my first thing, Miles. They took it. I've been trying to tell you, but I couldn't find a good time so I thought I'd make it a surprise."

"I see. And I never knew. So it's you who's been having this disastrous effect on me. You've enticed my Muse out of the study and had her shackled by your typewriter all this time. You villain. But well done. Marvellous. Bravo, my little Lizzie." He lay back on his pillows and clapped, smiling at her. "But I shan't read it now. I'll take it into my study when everyone's gone and clear my head with a large black coffee and give it the best of my formidable attention. Is it good?"

"I don't know, really. You'll have to tell me. I had to change a few bits for them."

"Yes, you sometimes do," said Miles, in the tones of one who knows that such things happen, but who has had the good fortune or talent to avoid them himself. His initial enthusiasm was already gone, and Elizabeth, who realized now that she had hoped her story would bring them closer again, thought she saw that he wasn't really pleased.

"And have you done others?"

"Yes. Two of them have been refused, and there are a couple I haven't heard about yet. Perhaps now I shall have the confidence to ring up and ask what's happening about them. And since that's been taken I've been working on something else, longer, which I think is going to be better."

"What about?"

"About . . . well, about a relationship," she said, lamely. "It's a sort of love story. It's turning out rather blacker than I meant it, and I have to work to keep it light, so it's going very slowly."

"Why black?"

"I'm not sure. I don't feel black, ordinarily, but somehow when I sit down and think about what I'm going to write, it comes out like that. I don't know why. Anyway—champagne."

Miles grabbed the bottle from the tray, shook it up and let the cork shoot to the ceiling. The pale liquid effervesced into the glass Elizabeth held out to him, and over her hand. She licked her fingers.

"To your twenty-five years, and all the others after," she said.

"To my twenty-sixth year. Keats died in his, you know. So could I, if I had written any masterpieces, quite happily."

"I don't suppose he knew they were masterpieces in quite that way."

"No, perhaps not. In that case, I shall console myself with the thought that my genius goes quite unrecognized."

"But it doesn't. Everybody recognizes it. You've got the most recognized genius in the country."

"Or the most over-recognized."

"Don't be morbid. Brilliant début, astonishing technique for one so young, etc., etc.—I quote . . ."

"Not so young any more. Pass me a croissant, will you?"

"When have you asked everyone to come?" She felt more cheerful. "Because you are going to have to come with me to collect the glasses I've ordered. There are two cardboard boxes, and I don't trust myself to manage them both."

"Right you are, ma'am. Rendezvous outside the bathroom in a quarter of an hour. No, make it half—I'm taking my glass with me and I don't want to waste the effect. I don't have champagne to drink every day in the bath, and it may give rise to novel impressions of the sort that lead to poetic inspiration. Half an hour and I shall be at your service. They're coming at half-past twelve, by the way. Or, at least, that's the *ante quam non*. The only person who will actually arrive then is Julius, in order to be polite, and that will mean, with any luck, that he will leave appropriately early and not bore the rest of us for hours."

With these brittle remarks, which showed Elizabeth that Miles was preparing to enjoy his birthday in extravagant fashion, he locked the bathroom door.

In Elizabeth's mind Miles's twenty-fifth birthday and the other one seven years later that sparked off the tragedy were to mingle inextricably. Not so much that they were similar—although she got very drunk at both of them—but because they seemed significant in a very particular way. The first marked her first success as a writer; the second the moment when she could no longer remain in any doubt about Miles. Of course, they had given other parties in between, but these, like the parties before, blurred together in a haze of general partiness: loud music, too many people, abortive conversations with guests whose names she couldn't remember about topics that didn't interest her. But these two parties kept clearer outlines. She could recall their beginnings, and—even though drunk—their ends, and scenarios from both repeated themselves to her in the traumatic weeks when she thought she would pull through and then decided she couldn't. From the first there was the gaiety of Miles during the preparations for the party, his gallantry on the short walk to and from the off-licence to collect the glasses, swinging from side to side of her as they crossed the roads to be between her and the kerb, and his mounting hilarity as he tossed salads and pulled corks. And half-way through the party, the moment when he stood, wobbling precariously, on a kitchen stool, clapped his hands and announced in stentorian tones that the first signs of literary genius had appeared in his wife. It was with difficulty that Elizabeth dissuaded him from reading her story aloud from his stool, but everyone had applauded her anyway, and in a strange way she had been pleased. That was the first party, an enormous success, when she had got drunk by mistake, as much with euphoria as with wine. The second party, though equally successful for everyone except herself, had been quite different. Miles had arrived home from his studio only twenty minutes before the first guest and had locked himself in the bathroom while the Swiss au pair girl arranged the quiches, the cold chicken and the home-made mayonnaise, and she piped Happy Birthday Miles 32 on his cake in chocolate squirts. As soon as the two children had been put to bed she started getting drunk, calculatingly, beginning with a stiff whisky, switching

133

to cider and then to red wine; in this state she slurred her words, but still noticed everything. She noticed how much more ingratiating people were these days, partly because of Miles's continued success, and partly because, with a novel recently under her belt, her own small reputation was expanding, too.

She noticed Julius leave with Miles's literary protégé, a young man who had just taken a brilliant first in Classical Mods and who wrote equally brilliant haiku. She noticed that the Swiss au pair girl looked left out, and introduced her to the wife of Miles's publisher, who could be relied upon to talk intelligently and charmingly. And she noticed, when she went upstairs to check that the children had not been woken by the noise, the buckle of the belt Miles was wearing that evening protruding from under the closed door of the spare room. Inside there was a scuffling, and laughter, a man's and a woman's. She had suspected it for a long time, and now she knew.

It was in her death that Elizabeth had revenge, although revenge was not what she had intended. On her part, it was a stroke of pure misery that refused to hold any further optimism within its grey grey edges. Miles was more surprised than anything else when the Swiss au pair rang the studio to tell him in her halting comic English that Elizabeth had gassed herself. It was some time since he had thought of her as an individual who might act autonomously. She was his wife, for God's sake: her life, though it didn't impinge very much on his own, was implicitly connected with his. When his surprise subsided, he was angry—had she realized what suspicions she would kindle in her parents and sisters and brother about his relationship with her? She had forgotten to leave a note explaining her motives, and he felt that his reputation as a son- and brother-in-law had been sullied; he had always been proud of his harmonious relationship with her family, so much better than his relationship with his own father. Then, as no one can be angry forever, he faced the most harrowing reaction: he wondered how she could possibly have felt strongly enough to do this to herself without his ever having noticed that something was wrong. He had thought that she might conceivably suspect his affair, but had been far from imagining that she might care so much about it. It worried Miles that the writer in him, for whom everything was subject-matter and the object of analysis, could have failed to spot so looming a subject as his own wife's misery in her life with him. He began to suspect that large parts of her character had remained a closed book to him in all the almost-ten years he had known her.

This suspicion grew and grew until it could no longer be called a suspicion and changed to an assurance on Miles's part. The friends of Elizabeth's who attended the funeral, or wrote to him, praised her kindness, her innate sympathy, her capacity for listening and for helping, qualities which—although he did not admit this—he had never noticed. But even stronger evidence of a breadth of personality far wider then he had ascribed to her came from her writing. Miles never knew—and he was tormented by this unknowable fact—whether it was by design or by mistake that he was made her literary executor. Had she forgotten to change her will, or had she left her first decision unchanged knowing that her writing would throw him into turmoil? He swung between the two views depending on his mood and the critical reaction that his own work was receiving. At the beginning, when his anger with her prevented objective thoughts about her work, he was still able to persuade himself that she had only been as good as he had first thought her. But slowly, as he forced himself to get through the short stories and poems she had left behind, to sort them and list them, even his insularity was not proof against the conclusion that she was almost always good, and sometimes brilliant. He was struck by the difference between her things and his. From the first he had been a great experimenter with styles and technique. His mind was a Catherine wheel which spun off exciting sparks of different colours, a great whirl of bravura whose point was itself. It was the way of saying rather than the

135

what that interested him. Her style had hardly changed in all the things she had written: everything stemmed from a core which was herself, her life and the incidents, small and not so small (but none of them very large), that had made it up.

Many of her stories had been woven like a rag rug from things they had done together. It intrigued him to see how much she could make of these episodes, how these small events of their life together could expand under her touch so that one day had become a paradigm for a whole period of their life, one conversation a passionate analysis of their relationship.

He was obsessed with what lay within her stories. He couldn't accept them, as strangers to her would, simply as stories: he searched inside them for her, for Elizabeth, for her ways of thinking and seeing, for the reasons why she saw things that way. Often in the first months after her death, when the children had been put to bed, he went up to her study, sat down at her desk, and took out of the drawer the manuscripts of her poems and prose. Sometimes he read them, but at others he merely sat and fingered them, looking at the shape of the letters—putting his hand on the paper as though to feel the imprint of the touch that her hands had left when she wrote. He sometimes felt a pang of loss.

The literary world felt a surge of interest in his wife's work once she was dead. Death in itself conferred a mythical stature, as though the stories spoke from beyond the grave with a stronger and truer voice than Elizabeth had possessed when she was alive.

Soon there was no one who did not know that Miles Davies had had a wife. In his more morose moments he thought there was a greater interest in her than in him, but as he was the sole possessor of many facts about her life, the interest was fairly divided. Her stories, much in demand now by literary magazines and women's magazines alike, sparked a curiosity to know all about her. What did she eat for breakfast? Was she a good cook? What was her favourite colour? How many words did she write a day? What were the children called? For a time Miles was happy to answer these questions. Perhaps his generosity in handing out rations of tiny detail to a voracious public was his way of atoning for the attention he hadn't paid her when she was alive. But after a time he came to resent being treated simply as the husband of Mrs Elizabeth Davies.

Thucydides

I expect you'd have mitched off school if you'd have been doing
Thucydides. You thought nobody did Greek any more, I
suppose? Well, when I was doing my A-levels, some people still
did: two of us, to be precise, and Thucydides was what we
started on. I don't know how much you know about
Thucydides. I had a love-hate relationship with him (that's a
cliché, I know, and perhaps I'll cut it out later, but at the
moment I'm just trying to tell you the story). The Penguin
translation I was using as a crib had something in the
introduction about his style being obscure. He certainly was
hellishly difficult at times. If he'd been alive today, he'd have
been the sort of man—an academic probably—who speaks in
inordinately long sentences, and who forgets half-way through
quite what the structure of his sentence is, so that it ends in a
way which is totally contradictory to the beginning. All very
well, you might think? Yes, but he wasn't speaking, he was
writing, so why didn't he correct himself afterwards? I never
quite figured it out.

But on the other hand he was a fascinating man. I don't know
whether you've seen Edward VI's diary in the British Museum,
the one who was Elizabeth's brother—I think he was sixteen
when he died? Well, it's full of figures, statistics I mean: lists of
all the cargoes coming into London with all the details of the
number of barrels of salt fish and ballast and the tonnage of each
vessel. He obviously had a passion for detail. I'm telling you this
because Thucydides was the same. When you read about the
battles in his War, you always knew how many people were on

138

each side, how many were cavalry and how many hoplites, and what sort of shields they had, so you could have made a film about it, there was so much information. If he could find out the exact details from people who were in the battle, he gave them to you. And if he couldn't find out exactly, he made them up, so they would fit in. I don't think that matters, do you? (Some people did. They said this was history, and history shouldn't be made up. But I had a good answer to that: that the Greek for history is the same as the Greek for story, which is true.) And then, if you're a girl—I am, and I never wanted to be—it's useful to find out how you stake a harbour-bottom to sabotage an incoming enemy fleet, and things of that sort. I became very interested in military tactics. Thucydides was a general himself at the beginning of the war, so you know he gets things right. Later on he was disgraced in some strange way which he never makes clear, and was exiled from Athens—that's one of the few details he doesn't give you.

So that's why I liked and didn't like Thucydides.

I don't think the problems started in my first A-level year. I worked very hard—of course I was doing other subjects as well as Greek. In the evenings after I came back from school we had tea and watched some television and then I went up to my room. I don't remember working on my other subjects, but I remember Thucydides. I had my book case on my left, opposite the bed, and my desk—only a table, really—next to that, with my volume of Thucydides and a vocabulary book and the two huge volumes of the Lidell and Scott dictionary. I worked slowly. At the beginning I was prepared to gloss over difficulties. I knew there was a lot I didn't *really* understand, and my vocabulary was small, and sometimes I had to look up almost every word in a sentence. But as I got better, I became more perfectionist. I would worry over a sentence for minutes, half an hour perhaps, until I not only understood the gist of what he was saying, but the relationship, grammatically, of every word to every other word in the sentence. And that was difficult, because Thucydides was so obscure, as I said before. Sometimes my father offered to help me, but I refused. He taught classics at the University, he was clever and a patient teacher, but I wanted to convince myself that I could cope with Greek on my own, without help.

So that was how the first year went. It was in the second year that things started going wrong. Not right at the beginning of the year, I think, but after a time I'd got myself into a hell of a mess. I had boy problems too, but I won't go into details over that. Like Thucydides I shall leave something out. It's always more interesting, don't you think, when a writer leaves something out? You can mull it over and wonder, and then it gives the critics a chance to have their different interpretations. Anyway, somehow I stopped working. It happened like this. One day, I hadn't had time to prepare any Greek. I felt guilty, and I didn't go to my class. Then the next class, I felt even guiltier—not only had I not prepared my Greek, but I hadn't gone to the previous class, and those two things together were harder to explain than either of them separately. So I didn't go to that class either. And so it went on, until it had escalated to such a point that I had to avoid my classics teacher in the school assembly hall, in the corridors, everywhere. So then I had to mitch off school. Perhaps it's not called mitching where you live, but that's what it's called in Swansea. It means staying away from school without having a letter from your parents to say that you were ill, or had to go to the dentist, or were looking so pale that your mother thought you surely *would* be ill, if she insisted on your taking that horrid long bus journey. I just mitched.

Perhaps I should have mentioned before that I lived in Swansea, but it's not really central to the story. Suffice it to say that it's where Dylan Thomas went to school—you probably know that. But now I'd better give a brief description of where we lived, because that will explain a few things. You probably think that descriptions are boring. I do too, but you see, I want

140

to be a writer later on, and writers always give descriptions at some point in the narrative, and so I think I should practise, and you'll have to bear with me.

When we came to Swansea, we looked at all sorts of different houses—old ones in the old parts, ones near the University and ones out beyond the Mumbles on Gower Peninsula, but what we chose was a hole in the ground. I mean that literally. By the time we came to move, the house was more or less finished, but when we first went to look at the site it was just a hole with a bulldozer in it amongst lots of other holes. So why did we choose it? Because of the view. If I were Tolstoy I could wax lyrical about that view. The house was almost at the brow of a hill which led on to a wild, marshy patch of common land where sometimes, in the very early morning, you saw foxes, and then to a golf course. The other way, towards the south, it looked over Swansea bay to the crooked Mumbles peninsula with its lighthouse and the coast of Devon beyond, and on the other side out towards the enormous Port Talbot oil refinery which grew plumes of smoke in the day time, and brilliant orange flames in the night, burning off the waste gases. It wasn't a view you would call sublime, I suppose, but it had something of everything, and it was never boring to look at. The sea was the best thing. In towns you tell the weather and the seasons by the greenness of plants and the times that flowers grow. But in Swansea you told the weather from the mood of the sea as well. The sea is more extreme. Sometimes an intense blueness with tiny foam-caps to each wave, but sometimes a thick angry oily grey, and enormous waves breaking over the sea wall at Mumbles and flooding the fishermen's cottages. I didn't realize how much I loved the sea until I left.

Then down the street and round the corner from the house was the park. It had been the grounds of a large house at the bottom of the park which now belonged to the University. It was a strange park, a bit fantastical. The people from the house must have had a good head-gardener, a man with a bizarre imagination. At the top, nearest our house, was an area of dogs' graves, about ten of them, all labelled with their names and dates, with daffodils and violets growing round them in the spring. Then there was a long wide sweep of grass that ran straight down the hill to the sea road. On one side was the big house, on the other a wood, and beyond that an area with a curious winding stream planted thickly with rhododendrons that grew luscious jungle flowers of red and white and dark pink. In one place there was a folly, and in another a sort of Chinese pagoda with a Chinese bridge crossing a pond covered with water lilies. Nothing could have been more incongruous in a park in Swansea, and it was one of my favourite places.

I said that this description was going to help you understand how things happened, and this is why. Every morning we walked through that park down the grass slope to the sea road where we waited for the bus to school. We is myself and my brothers and sister. I forgot to tell you until now that I had any brothers or sisters—it didn't seem necessary because this story is really about me, and a little about my father. But I just wanted you to know that I wasn't an only child, in case you thought in that ridiculous Freudian way that it was because I was an only child that I worked so hard and let the work get on top of me and then had to mitch off school. So usually we walked together and caught the bus together, but sometimes one or other of us went early, to play football before school started, or copy someone's homework if we hadn't had time to do it the night before, or it had been too difficult. When I got into this dreadful muddle at school it didn't seem odd to any of them that I started getting up a bit earlier and going off to catch an earlier bus. In fact, that isn't what I was doing. I walked down to the park gates, turned right just inside the fence and walked to the Chinese pagoda. If it was sunny I sat on the steps leading down to the pool, and if it was raining I sat inside the pagoda. Sometimes I spent the whole morning there reading. You mustn't think that I was lazy, and that that was why I mitched. It was just that Thucydides was so obscure. I said just now that I want to be a writer, and probably already then I had an idea that that was what I wanted to be, so I read voraciously, especially poetry. But if it was very cold, I couldn't bear a whole morning in the pagoda, and I timed on my watch, carefully, the times when everyone should have left the house—my brothers and sister to my school, my mother to the junior school where she taught, and my father to the University, plus half an hour for all eventualities (the car breaking down, or someone oversleeping). Then I went back up through the park to the house, let myself in and spent the rest of the day in comfort in my room.

Well, this is where we get to the main point of the story, where you will see how indirectly Thucydides was the cause of my discovering something awful. If he hadn't made his Peloponnesian War so difficult to read, I don't suppose I ever would have discovered, and if I hadn't discovered I probably would not have done a lot of things I did afterwards. Because the discovery made me change my views about a great many things. If you were going to be Freudian about things, you would probably say that it caused my transition from puberty to adulthood. And everyone knows how painful that transition is.

It was late spring by this time, but in Swansea the spring, instead of bringing the first fine weather and being the harbinger of summer, was often the beginning of a rainy season that I sometimes thought couldn't be much worse than the monsoons. As the alarm went off in the morning you were immediately aware of the constant sound of water, falling from the sky, pouring down the gutters and the drains and in streams down the road. The lawns in front and behind the house were water-logged, the trees sprouted moulds on their trunks, and in the park it was difficult to avoid the slugs there were so many. On this particular morning the rain was so heavy I considered not leaving the house at all, but that would have been dangerous, and I got myself up and to the park in the end.

I don't know why, but when I got back to the house, my

father's car was still in the drive. Perhaps I hadn't allowed the full extra half an hour—it was so wet and I was so cold. The only thing to do was to wait in the garage until he left, and that's what I did. It was a case of making the best of a bad job. Some people's garages are so neat you could quite happily live in them, but our's wasn't one of those. The old book case of my grandfather's, with its jam-jars full of rusting nails and screws, tins of oil and coils of fuse-wire, was the neatest thing in it. The rest was a chaotic jumble—the lawn-mower and the step-ladder, tools and a flat tyre—and there was hardly enough light coming through the one low window to read by. So I simply sat, listening to the rushing rain, and through that for the scraping of the front door against the metal door-sill, which would signal my father's departure. After almost half an hour the rain seemed to ease off a little, and then the door scraped and I heard the clicking of my father's shoes—he had recently taken to wearing a pair of old-fashioned black lace-up shoes, with metal half-moons at the back of the heel to stop them wearing down. But then as I stood up and tried to rub the pins and needles out of my legs, I thought I heard other footsteps. I probably wouldn't have been sure—the rain was still swirling down the gutters—but then I heard voices. One was my father's; the other a woman's voice, not my mother's.

"Get in," he said. "I'll drive you to the bus-stop."

"Couldn't you take me all the way? I've got a class at eleven and the weather's filthy."

"Sorry. We might be seen. You really shouldn't have come here either. It was a stupid thing to do."

"I had to. I was miserable after yesterday evening and I thought you might . . ."

Her voice trailed off, the doors slammed, and after some damp rumblings the engine started up and the car reversed up the drive and then down the hill. The quietness of the rain flowed slowly back and I stared blankly at the rust on the back of the garage door. I thought of my mother starting on the third lesson of the day on the other side of the town.

It was at the end of that week that the school telephoned my parents to tell them that I hadn't been to school for some weeks. I must have suspected that things were coming to a head. I had gone to bed with a slight temperature and the beginnings of a cold, a real one, but one which stemmed not so much from sitting in the damp garage as from my state of mind, which was as dismal as the weather. My parents came up separately to talk to me. My mother remonstrated quietly, and my father lectured me slightly. I cried. He thought I was crying about Thucydides, in repentance for the work I hadn't done. But I was crying about him. I was seeing things in a different perspective, and Thucydides didn't seem so much of a problem as he had before.

Helen Harris

THE LIZARD BEHIND THE LAVATORY CISTERN
SEA VIEW
THE OTHER LAUNDERETTE

The Lizard behind the Lavatory Cistern

The lizard must live behind the lavatory cistern. He always ran
back there if she hissed at him. She didn't hiss often. Mainly
they just stared, Anna and the lizard, trying to outdo each
other's rigid gaze. But occasionally, out of boredom, or perhaps
because she thought he was winning, she would hiss loudly to
restore her dominance and gloat as he dashed away. It wasn't a
fair battle but Anna was glad that she could at any rate impress
someone in India.

The lizard was a personality although she didn't name him.
That would be belittling, colonial. "Hello, Reptile Sahib, good
evening." "Ah, Lizardji, we meet again." No, he was the lizard
and partly because he was such a big one, Anna felt that they
were actually equals. He occupied his share of the hotel room
just as convincingly as she did hers. He was a custardy shade of
yellow while most other lizards were green. In the mornings, he
would sometimes wake her with his urgent dashes across the
ceiling. If she looked up at him for long enough and the fever
was there, they became interchangeable. Anna was the reptile,
splayed out on her clammy sheets—"Ah, you English, you are
so cold"—and he was warm-blooded and active, going about his
affairs. She wondered what the room must look like to him; she
would wag her head and watch the walls tilt, imagining she
crawled along the cornice. She looked down from there at the
creature on the bed and she exclaimed into the silence, "Why
are you still waiting? Where is he?"

When they first met in England at a drinks do, he had said to
her ponderously, "I think maybe they called you Anna because

149

you are so small." She knew nothing about India then—she had
no reason to—and he needed to explain a bit awkwardly about
an anna being an old kind of coin, worth very little, and as he
dealt with that aspect of it, he floundered. Afterwards, he had
apologized about that laborious beginning, when they knew
each other better, when they could make fun of the obvious. She
had referred to it herself later; she asked him jokingly, but with
suppressed anxiety (in bed), "Well, I hope you don't think now
I'm called Anna because I'm cheap." He had pulled her head
under his armpit and laughed and laughed. Because she spent so
much time in bed here, she remembered a lot of things like that.

She lay and looked at the lavatory cistern. It had more
significance than providing a home for the lizard. It epitomized
a whole era of cultural domination; cumbersome and white,
"Shanks Prize Medal Reliable No. 16A". She had not expected
it and, after twirling the long brass chain and laughing at it, she
had expected even less that it would soon become a welcome
landmark, a compatriot in alien confusion. "Ha," he had said,
"a museum piece. A panacea for some Collector's piles." She
saw it constantly through the open door and she had infinite
time to interpret its symbolism and marvel at how sturdily it had
survived. Some feet below the cistern, the bowl had not done as
well; orange stains had spread up from the floor and at some
time, the original seat had been replaced by a shoddy one, which
sat askew on the solid pedestal. The bathroom should have been
quintessentially English. But the climate or something had
turned it into a startling travesty. Anna knew that an English
bathroom was the smallest, dreariest room in a house, a
cubby-hole, which put washing low as a national concern. But
this bathroom was palatial and furnished as though it would be
inhabited. There was a mirrored wardrobe to the left of the
door. In this mirror, Anna had seen her illness for the first time,
grey-green and wavering in the uneven glass. The hotel laundry
list, pinned to the old wood of the wardrobe, enumerated the
different charges for washing sarees, dhotis, kurtahs and

pyjamas. It led her to imagine previous occupants of the room and, by and large, that was a good thing. She imagined skinny couples fussing together over their laundry beside the yellowing list. They were mainly elderly and finicky about their food, insisting on having vegetarian meals brought up for them by the room boy. She listened to the sound of their early morning washing; thorough hawking and spitting into the cavernous basin. Once the husband of the least appealing couple, whose name was Habibullah, soaped his soft bulk caressingly as he stood in the bathtub singing a guttural song. She wondered, while the listless shower seeped over her, whether the Habibullahs had speculated about their predecessors; angular English couples in the thirties, who had maybe occasionally indulged in a frivolous joint bath. Of course, the lizards did away with the bathroom's English pretensions and so did the bright green and crimson strands of the garden, which scraped intermittently at the mosquito mesh. But nothing undermined the bedroom. Its window opened on to the veranda. It was always shadowy and remote. At first, Anna had cried there because it was so ludicrously distant from what she had come for.

The two of them had spoken frequently about her trip to India, funnily enough even before their acquaintance had advanced the way it had. "But of course you must come," he had answered repeatedly. "You will stay with our family. It will be marvellous." Later, naturally, the character of her trip had changed; the romantic overtones and complications had not seriously detracted from the enjoyment. Probably, the biggest change was in her own eagerness; it was his laugh, his face, his presence she looked forward to, not alienation and the weird buildings and the sun. She was coming now as part of their experiment, she was coming to be with him.

"Number Eight", the receptionist had declared, "is a very fine room." And eight was such a neutral, bland number, especially after the more disturbing revelations, which had brought her to the hotel, that she felt no curiosity as she stood behind the elderly porter and he scrabbled to unlock the double doors. A huge padlock bound them together. When he eventually undid it, there was another flimsier pair of doors behind. "Very *good*," said the porter, as if he sensed her doubt but attributed it to the fittings of the hotel. He flung the inner doors open quite recklessly so that Anna should walk in in style but she felt so indifferent, already so sullen towards the place, that she did not see. When the wizened porter stepped in front of her and announced, "I am your boy," it did not occur to her that it might be funny.

She spent every day in the bedroom. At first, she had made the effort to go down for meals in the large, empty dining room. But since the fever, she found she could no longer predict her reactions to plates of orange vegetable. Orange like the earth. The air seemed fetid and the thin waiters circled around her table. She took to ordering her food on the telephone, even though it took an hour or two to come. A strangled voice from a long way off would query, "Eight, madam?" And she would cry, "No, no, I said egg, you know, egg." After a long, offended silence, the voice would reply, "I am sorry, madam. I am not understanding you."

He would not have stood for it. One of his less admirable qualities was his lordliness, the loud, curt way he dealt with inferiors. He thought they were inferiors. He would have seized the telephone receiver and brusquely hectored them in Hindi. He would have called her "Muddlehead" and would have referred to them as "these people".

Then, later, when she had forgotten what it was she had asked for so passionately and was sometimes asleep, a knock would come at the outer bedroom door and a short figure would totter in with a giant tray on his shoulder. She ate sitting on the floor. The fact that her meals were brought on a tray and that she sat on a fancy, if worn carpet was completely irrelevant. She considered sitting on the floor a wonderfully Indian act. In this pompous, old bedroom, she scooped up her food with her fingers. All the things she had taken to rather joyously in India—sitting on the floor, throwing off her shoes, eating with her fingers—he more or less disdained. Still, that was to be expected. From the floor, the bedroom acquired a humbler perspective. The big brown furniture looked stranded and extinct. Broken springs dangled out of the seat of the armchair. Ants marched under the writing desk where, on the first day, she had been delighted to find the Bible was infested with insects, because it was so satisfyingly symbolic. She had in a dismal sort of way got used to being here. But, none the less, it was awful to be kept at arm's length by India when she had come here intending to embrace it.

During the day, a series of small men would come into the bedroom; to change the towels, the drinking water, to sweep. Anna thought they were frightened of her. They would scuttle in, holding their faces stiffly away so that they didn't see her scanty nightdress, and this increased her feeling of being a monster, directing them with her yellow arms. It wasn't at all difficult to tell them apart but because she was weak, she distinguished them by their jobs; here comes the lavatory brush, the tea. She thereby lapsed unconsciously into a parody of the caste system. She liked the lavatory brush best because he tended the bathroom shrine. He was a bandy-legged old man with protruding eyes, which looked in different directions. This made him seem particularly frightened. When he had scrubbed the lavatory and ceremonially pulled the chain, he ran from the room. Anna found that she was being patronizing, in spite of her original intentions.

On the aeroplane, she said exuberantly to the Indian businessman beside her, "I'm going to stay with my boyfriend." He asked which city he lived in and what was his name. "Oh," he said when he heard, "*Indian* boyfriend," and, after that remark, his attitude seemed to develop quickly. He was intrigued and admiring, but also somehow too jovial. When she woke up before Abu Dhabi, he was blatantly appreciating her breasts.

If it hadn't been for that sort of thing, Anna might have sat out more often on the veranda. Broad cane chairs faced the garden and all her favourite wildlife, chipmunks, hoopoes, as well as gorgeous butterflies, zigzagged about. Inside, of course, she had the fan, whirling and creaking until it seemed certain to fly down and scythe her to bits. But the cool of the fan alone was not enough of a reason; it was the inevitable, sly way that onlookers would assemble if she sat outside that discouraged her. It took about twenty minutes from whenever the first gardener saw her for most of the others to have found work in the same patch of garden. If she looked up, their heads would be bowed, but they saw her all the same. Pretty soon, one of the aged room boys would come and offer her tea or fruit juice or some snack and then there was no longer need for any pretence; all the hotel staff and the gardeners would come close, listen to the conversation, nodding their heads and staring at her and smiling.

He had met her at Delhi airport, at six o'clock on a dazzling morning. It had seemed to her an awkward, perilous time to arrive but, in fact, everything was functioning as if it was midday. They went to a small hotel near New Delhi Station. Anna would have been frightened if she had had to stay there alone. She was so exhausted and bemused after the flight, she went straight to bed. But she couldn't sleep and so he undressed and joined her. She did not see a great deal of Delhi. It was so awful every time they went outside; she had to remember not to touch him, not even hands, and kissing or lolling in a park were quite out of the question. Not that there seemed to be many parks near their hotel. All the same, there were looks and sly comments. Men would walk against her too clumsily for it to be accidental. But he said, "Oh come now," when she started to complain. "It's an overcrowded country." Despite all her plans and guidebooks and his warnings that there would be nothing much to see when they got to his home town, she frankly preferred to stay in the hotel where at least they could be normal. She enjoyed easier aspects of the country; fresh limes, an orange-and-green silk shawl, his touch. She knew they would be separated at his parents.

The old hotel was the second grandest in the town. Somewhere else, there was a more modern one and that was where foreigners stayed. Anna was not entirely exaggerating the attention she aroused; she was a curiosity. The other guests, perhaps a dozen of them, were wealthy, middle-aged Indians. Sometimes they would accost her summarily on the veranda, "Which country you are coming from?" and demand why she was staying there, what had brought her to the town? Although his visits always took place in the daytime, they still seemed to cause disapproval. In the room next door to Anna's was an industrialist with his stunningly fat wife, who would stroll up and down the veranda, taking exercise, and cast hostile looks at Anna's window each time she passed. Anna began to understand why he arrived in such an irritable state and exclaimed that the hotel staff had recognized him, everyone knew his family here, that this situation was becoming intolerable, that it could not go on.

What had shocked her most about his family? Was it the relative simplicity of their house, although they were so well off? Or was it the casualness, really verging on apathy, with which his parents greeted her, which made it quite clear, after a couple of days, that they thought she was just another of their son's English friends, who was passing through on a sightseeing tour of the East? Gradually, she suspected that his mother disapproved of her. She didn't talk much anyway, but when Anna was there, she became absolutely silent, staring down at her silk lap. At first, this cheered Anna because it surely implied that she took her presence seriously. But, in due course, she decided it was just her independence that his mother disapproved of and she could not envisage any connection between

155

Anna and her son at all. His father liked to talk to her, a bit dogmatically, it was true, but that was better than being left with the women. The main problem was that there was actually nothing to do. People didn't seem to have hobbies or read books. Once Anna had been taken shopping and to a few rather dull places, which passed for the sights, she was expected to be content to idle. He had warned her, of course. "It won't be all fun and games in my family," he had said, "you'll have to compromise a bit." But she had thought that everything would work out somehow once she got there.

He was right; it was a dull town. But, although it wasn't large, it seemed to comprise three or four totally different districts. At first, Anna had thought it was all like the broad streets around his house. Then, when they had been out to the bazaar, she assumed it was sharply divided into rich and poor. But the area where the old hotel was turned out to be quite different yet again and she wondered if she had understood anything at all. The hotel stood in a portion called the Civil Lines. It embarrassed her even to say it; it was so reminiscent of the era of the lavatory cistern. The buildings were white and heavy; now they were local government offices and the bank. There were white walls around gardens and shadows crouched at the gates. Was it a very typical town? Would there be an old hotel like this in most others? If she were in another city, in love with another tall Brahmin BA, would this still have happened?

It was impossible now to say what had prompted the fight. All the causes seemed so small. The evening before, everyone had eaten some special dish made with curds, apparently affably. His mother was already weeping when Anna woke up. The argument hadn't been helped, certainly, by the family's incredible lack of self-restraint. Even his silent mother sobbed and shrieked and you could hear her clearly right through the house. Anna didn't dare come out of the room she shared with Cousin Praba. But she got very thirsty after a while and went downstairs. She thought she would never forget his mother's

156

face as she saw Anna. Her mouth opened wide around a desperate howl and then, screwing up her features into an unrecognizable bundle, she pointed Biblically at her and screamed. He had not been all that restrained himself. But this was in her defence. She could forgive him his tears. His father had erupted arbitrarily into the fight, bullying them both, apparently unable to sense that this was a dispute he could not settle with his authority. It had been like this all along, of course. In the middle of a quiet discussion, his father might shout, "Coffee!" and, at once, coffee would become the focus of attention. Or, worse, he might command, "Everyone drink coffee," like some curious party game and all the family would have to troop into the room where he sat and sip coffee, chatting together and smiling. That day, he had bellowed, impotently, for every time he intervened, another member of the family started to shout. It lasted for hours. The household's shaky routine, fragile at the best of times, collapsed. Because of the length of the row and the varied number of people involved, from time to time Anna came across a quiet individual eating *rotis* in the midst of the disruption. The worst of it was not being able to understand exactly what was going on; seeing all their tortured, tearful faces and not knowing if it was really her or something quite unconnected which they were so upset about. She had such an uncertain idea of who thought what that when he came into her room and said, "Pack. You have to go," she wondered for a minute whose decision it was. "Pack," he had repeated. "Where are your things?" and then he had stood there, explaining, while she hectically filled her suitcase, crying now too. "It is the only way," he said. "You must see that." She should pretend to leave but go to this hotel he had thought of. She could stay there until they found an alternative and he would come to visit. She supposed, very briefly, that she should have gone; taken a train back to Delhi and a plane to London. But, my goodness, she had known it would not be easy here. How could she have given up then?

So she came to the hotel on a cycle rickshaw, holding her suitcase on to the narrow seat, and the shaven rickshaw man, with one last, little tuft of hair on his head so that his god could pull him up to heaven when he died, out of the awfulness of India, kept gaping round at her, pedalling conscientiously because he did not know what else to do.

Sea View

At seven thirty on the morning of September the first, the roadworks began again. The municipality had decreed, after repeated complaints by worried hoteliers, that for the month of August the drilling was to stop. On the fine morning of September the first, the pastel walls of the boarding houses near the sea were shaken from their cocoon again. The tree-lined streets, intersecting at tidy right angles, were so toytown-like and placid, the sudden roar of the drilling seemed like an outburst of spiteful temper that anywhere should be so serene. But by the first of September, only rare and perhaps eccentric guests were left in the boarding houses. They were either unsuccessful holiday-makers, who had no idea of standing up for their rights, or those of such tremendous privilege in having extra leisure time that the municipality felt it their positive duty to remind them there were other people in the world less fortunate.

The bedrooms of the Villa Olga rebounded at the first thrust of the drills. Outside, the sunshine was making a queasy colour experiment on the ochre walls. Lunch was still dewy and unpeeled in the garden. The roadworks would have none of it.

Cordelia awoke with a start behind the perforated shutters and felt in the yellow half-light for her watch. When she saw it was not even twenty-five to eight, she cursed and let the watch fall in exasperation. She had come all this way to be woken only fifteen minutes later than she would have to get up at home. She lay for a minute, absorbing the injustice and the prospect of the day on the unfamiliar sheets. Her

159

watch started to chatter on the glass of the bedside table.

Cordelia was not a privileged holiday-maker. She had come to Miramare in September because she had no alternative. Those of her colleagues at the museum with school-age children had first choice of holiday dates, wielding their children ruthlessly in the administrative bargaining. Those married to schoolteachers also had a strong claim. But Cordelia, having neither children nor husband, as one of them was always bound to point out, could take her holiday at any time. This year, she had chosen Italy. They had rolled their eyes heavenwards at the museum, murmuring about the Uffizi, Ravenna and the mosaics, to compensate for their selfishness over the dates. But Cordelia wanted an utter holiday, for once, and so she had decided on Miramare where there was nothing but the boarding houses and the beach.

The Villa Olga had been recommended to her by the married brother of a friend, who commented privately that he thought it a little peculiar, Cordelia going off there on her own like that. She wanted to lie in the sun, rub oil into her still lean, long body, eat substantial, ritual meals and sleep in late. She packed her lightweight suitcase with bikinis, a number of enjoyable paperback books and a floral sundress. She also took precautions, in case of a light-hearted holiday encounter.

The Villa Olga did not seem a likely setting for that sort of mischief. It stood on the corner of two neat streets in its snug vegetable garden, one of the colony of little *petit four* villas. Pink, pale green and coffee, they portrayed an innocent, sugary version of life, which never had to confront upheaval or winter weather. For the short, sunny stretch of its existence, nothing was allowed to disrupt its cherished round of breakfast, lunch and dinner.

When her taxi stopped at the low gates, Cordelia's resolve had almost faltered, her determination to have a totally blithe, mindless holiday in front of the waves. Wasn't this precisely what she spent her time in England fighting off? This was

smugness and stultification, painted to look appealing. Whatever character she allotted herself, she would be out of place
here. Gauche, fine-ankled, she stepped out of the taxi.

The first evening was a bit depressing, eating pasta and veal
stew in the plain dining room. The other guests were un-
promising: two Italian families with over-disciplined, solemn
children, an elderly couple who scarcely spoke, a priest.
They all politely avoided looking at her. The landlady, who
served the food herself, brought Cordelia's solicitously, heaving
her large bosom tactfully above the tray. It was clear that she
found her new guest puzzling and pitiful and had decided to
treat her like a person bereaved. Cordelia left the dining room
feeling mollycoddled, an invalid on her way up to an early night.

And now, this morning, the drilling, the hideous repeated
drilling, shaking the shutters and the tawdry little Madonna and
Child by the washbasin. She did hope this holiday was not going
to be a mistake.

Cordelia was forty-two. Depending on her state of mind and
the weather, she could look a lot younger or somewhat older,
but the fact that she was forty-two was important to her. It
affected both her actions and her attitudes to other people.
When she was twenty-two, she did not remember thinking, "I
can't do this; I'm twenty-two." Now, she caught herself
thinking it more and more often. She had a distinct image of a
forty-two-year-old woman and she felt she bore little relation to
it. On the one hand, this was a source of perverse pride. On the
other, she had an intermittent coward's craving to conform. She
had wondered if she was too old for this kind of holiday. Now
she thought maybe she was too young.

The Villa Olga sat in the morning sunshine and submitted to
the drills with dignity. The landlady set out uneventful white
rolls in baskets on the dining-room tables. (Her name was
actually not Olga, but Amelia. She had bought the name Olga
with the villa from her White Russian Milanese predecessor and
she had kept it for commercial reasons.) In all the streets of the

colony, there was an intimate smell of coffee. There were only freaks, as yet, on the beach.

Quite solemnly, the first morning, Cordelia packed up her suntan lotion and towel and went down to the beach. At the back of her head, an insidious, plummy voice made fun of her. But she spread her towel on the sand and unscrewed the cap of her suntan lotion. A few yards away, the children from the Villa Olga eyed her with stern disbelief. She gave them a courteous, though unappreciated good morning and began to rub in her lotion with relish. By lunchtime, she was a nice preparatory coral and she could feel the first gratifying warmth of sunburn.

In the afternoon, she slept, waking intermittently to remember untied ends of her English life. The Villa Olga was imposingly quiet, though occasionally someone visited the lavatory in the corridor. It was just the end of the lunch hour at the museum; she would be returning from lunch in the canteen, or the wine bar, with Cyril and Jonathan and Mr Waite. Jonathan would flirt with her expansively on the stairs, genially make fun of Mr Waite. She wondered briefly how their work on the exhibition catalogue was going but suppressed the thought quickly for she was on holiday. After lunch, they would all potter ineffectually through the afternoon, working in a desultory way. Jonathan would pass her door for eternal cups of coffee, stopping on his way back to chat until they cooled down. Cyril never stopped to chat with her, although his office was nearer; she heard his plummy voice proclaim his self-sufficiency in a series of personal telephone calls. She knew they were personal from his hectoring, debonaire tone. In museum matters, he was always quiet and deferential. Mr Waite dictated letters to his secretary in a high-pitched, breathless bray. How the little girl restrained her laughter, Cordelia always wondered. Her colleagues found Cordelia fun, an easy-going type, who, with no obvious obstacles, should have got married long ago. This, they assumed, was why she sometimes became unhealthily over-anxious about her work.

Sea View

From the museum, she went home, reading on the number 73 bus, and, at home, another untied end was waiting for her; the flat she shared with a girl called Janice. She and Janice had begun sharing flats at a time when they could both reasonably still be called girls and the passing years had left them stranded in the high-ceilinged, unheated flat. Their friends had married or got too set in their solitary ways to share. Yet Janice and Cordelia did not like each other. Periodically, from their early thirties onwards, one of them, almost always Cordelia, would raise the question of moving, each finding their own flat, and, for a while, they would hunt. But inevitably, one of them, almost always Janice, gave up; it was too depressing, prices were too high. And they would go on bickering and halving the kitchen cupboards. Cordelia had long felt that Janice was retaining her in the outgrown arrangement. A teacher in an all-girls school, she had got used to this lopsided life. Every time Cordelia went away, she resolved to move out when she got back.

The next time she woke up, she thought about her father. Was it the smell in the closed bedroom, grown musty, which had reminded her of the little room he occupied in an old people's home in Bournemouth?

At five o'clock, she got up and, spurning the bidet, washed laboriously at the washbasin. She put on her nicer dress and squirted scent behind her ears. It was time for an aperitif.

In the evening, there was soup and a breaded cutlet for dinner and afterwards she took a walk along the illuminated seafront.

The next morning, there was no drilling but Cordelia woke with a jump at half-past seven, expecting it. Instead there was an intermittent hammering, which stopped just long enough for her to fall back into sleep and then clouted her awake again. She lay there in the incomplete darkness and envisaged a day, which was a straightforward repetition of yesterday, but seemed less agreeable. Perhaps she would walk along to find a nice new spot on the beach.

The drilling resumed during breakfast but by a convention of bravado, everyone ignored it. The coffee cups rattled on their wide saucers. One of the Italian children giggled at them and was rebuked. What dreadful, repressive parents, Cordelia thought, destroying all spontaneity and appreciation of phenomena in their children. She examined the two families furtively across the dining room and saw two similar sets of well-dressed parents, too well-dressed for a seaside holiday, and their clean, unhappy young. In one family, there was a small daughter and two sons, in the other, just two sons. She registered their sallow, expressionless faces and their smooth dark hair. She recognized the two boys of the family without a girl as the children who had stared at her on the beach the day before. They sat solidly at their coffee as if they would never leap up and rush squealing into the sea. Cordelia condemned their father, who imposed his fussy, moustached tyranny from the head of the table and despised their smart mother, who was suffering ostentatiously from the quality of the coffee.

She chose her new spot on the beach, midway between the jetty and the parasol-hire man. It was some way down from the Villa Olga and so she was surprised, when she sat up after an hour or so to renew her suntan lotion, to notice one of the boys from the boarding house sitting not far off. It was one of the two brothers again. Watching him unobserved as she put on her lotion, Cordelia realized that this one was not actually a child; he had no roundness any more, his shoulders made a determined shape. He must be thirteen or fourteen years old. Away from his family group, she perceived him clearly for the first time. He was a sullen boy, that much she had got right; he had a dark, solemn face and the way he sat sternly, almost ignoring the frivolous sand around him, expressed a severe judgement of everyone else on the beach. Examining him with a mild interest, Cordelia now saw he was not crushed by his parents' discipline. His gloom was cultivated, not a child's apathetic acceptance of forces beyond his control. He had chosen to sit here alone, far from his family, and his silhouette said he was aloof. She changed her position from front to back. How easy it was to mis-interpret someone totally, she thought, before relapsing into her sweltering coma.

Later, she looked up and he had gone. She wondered if his small-minded father had come puffing down the beach while she had her eyes shut and summoned him back with a humiliating display of authority.

At lunch, she looked across at their table once or twice. During her siesta, she realized that becoming harmlessly interested in the other guests at the Villa could be a way of combatting the place's incipient dullness. On her way into dinner, after two Martinis at a café on the front, she spoke to the priest and asked him where in Italy he came from. He was startled and not especially pleased at being spoken to. He threw himself at his food when she left him alone, like a solution.

Throughout the meal, a disagreement festered uncomfort-ably in the family with the little girl. Cordelia could not understand exactly what was going on; the father frowned, the mother sighed, the three children sat rigidly and shovelled their spaghetti. In an automatic comparison, she glanced at the other family. They were eating in a silent truce. The boy from the beach was covertly watching the argument at the other table with an expression of dry, cynical familiarity on his face.

She looked out for him the next day on the beach and was almost disappointed not to catch sight of him. It was another warm day, but a slight breeze and cloud spoiled the sunbathing. After lunch, not feeling like lying down in her dark room, she went down on to the veranda to read in one of the cane chairs. He was there. He was sitting on the step with a book but staring out into the vegetable garden, what seemed like contempt for the runner beans and carrots on his face. Cordelia noticed he had changed his neat mealtime clothes for a pair of aged shorts, out of which his lean, brown legs sprouted defiantly. She sat down quietly in one of the fraying old chairs and opened her book. It was already her second book of the holiday and the amount she had been reading had sapped her concentration. After a little while, she looked over at the boy and, not surprisingly, he was looking at her. His eyes dropped instantly, but since he had had to turn slightly to see her, his movement was obvious.

She went on looking at him for a minute or two and took in some new, unrelated details; his haircut was like a helmet, too severe for his slender neck, his long toes were clenched around lumps of gravel. She looked back at her book. (In a snug village in the Home Counties, the local pageant was providing the pattern for a florid knitting of emotions and intrigue.) Again, she looked up, again his eyes dropped. This time, she saw herself in her cane chair as he must see her; a strange, foreign lady, prowling somehow around his peaceful afternoon. She shuffled uncomfortably. It was patently her duty, as the adult, to get them out of this impasse. Hurriedly, she called, unpremeditated, "Are you having a good holiday?" She hated the sound of her voice when she spoke Italian, the affected prancing of an English finishing school. "Are you having a good holiday?"

He looked round. Was she a patronizing parent or a conspirator? In her eagerness to show him that she was a conspirator, Cordelia rolled her eyes disparagingly at the garden, included the house and its occupants in her scorn. The boy replied, "What does it look like to you?"

If he had said nothing, if he had quite understandably let her question shrink into silence, things would have gone no further; without any encouragement, her curiosity could have been diverted to someone else.

"I thought as much," said Cordelia. "It's very sleepy here, isn't it?"

"Sleepy?" said the boy. "I would say moribund." And there was something immediately endearing to Cordelia in this childish overstatement, the kind of brash accusation she would

166

like to make, but now felt she was too old (forty-two).

"What are you reading?" she asked, aware at once that she must sound like a schoolteacher, quizzing him.

He flicked the pages of his book dismissively. "*The Catcher in the Rye* by J. D. Salinger," he said. "It's not up to much."

"In English?" Cordelia asked ingratiatingly. It was an effort for her to think of appropriate things to say too.

He quivered with slight irritation. "In translation."

"Does your family come here every year?" she asked.

He drew himself up. "This is the last year that I'm coming on holiday with them," he declared. "Next year, I will be free." He made a brusque, demonstrative gesture at the fruit cage. "Next year I will buy an Inter-Rail pass and travel round Europe."

"Oh my," said Cordelia, "that would be wonderful." To prove her sincerity, she added, "I'd love to do that myself. But of course I'm too old. The age limit's twenty-six, isn't it?"

He gave her a frank stare; gracious, that old. They both broke into hesitant laughter, but stopped quickly at the sound of footsteps in the house, as though whoever it was would surely disapprove.

Later on, it struck Cordelia that their conversation had been entirely one way—he had not asked for a single piece of information about her—but eventually she thought that was natural in a conversation between a grown-up and a schoolboy.

That evening, in the dining room, the boy was again stonily part of his family tableau. He did not glance over at Cordelia and speared his food vindictively as usual. His father complained to the landlady that there was veal cutlet on the menu again. She barely thought about him in her bedroom, wrote two postcards, read, and she was genuinely startled when she woke in the depths of the night with indigestion to find him at the front of her thoughts. What is more he was lithe and brown and alluring and she was drawn to him. As the layers of sleep lifted, she realized in confusion that she had been painting the boy the way she had painted only three or four particular grown men before.

167

She felt a moment of frank self-congratulation; someone new to play with. But at once the familiar lordly voice reproved her.

Perhaps like other women with sparse companions, her imaginary company was plentiful and bold. (In the days when she and Cyril had gone home together from the museum, she had been wonderfully happy, but she had lost her imagination. Her unattainable fantasies of so many afternoons were realized, but her imagination was bare. With Cyril blond and naked in her shower after love, she lay alone and sometimes tried to regenerate those visions. But her energy must have been diverted; she could no longer recall those gorgeous, tumultuous possibilities which had transformed her green office, and she missed them.) Now, to her shock and shame, she found herself thinking in that way about the boy.

She rolled over. Gracious, she was old enough to be his mother. (That was the comment which people would inevitably make.) Maybe this was a foiled maternal instinct emerging in an unexpected shape. Did she want to cuddle the boy because, subconsciously, she wished she had mothered him? In the dark, she had to grin. It was too preposterous. She was simply trying to put a respectable motive to her desire; she knew it was a red herring. *Faute de* Cyril—even half-asleep, she chided herself, she spoke the language of her class—*faute de* Cyril, her imagination had set on the boy. Restlessly, she shifted and stretched to ease her indigestion. She looked resentfully at the luminous fingers of her travelling alarm clock. They could be saying half-past three or half-past four; it was that sort of clock. She would have to reach right out of bed to be sure and, wide awake, Lord knows how she would have judged her drowsy fantasies. She lay quite still. Through waves of sleepiness, she let the boy come up to her again across the beach, smile affectionately and sit down beside her. They shivered in the sun. She drew his hand from next to him and guided it gently under her neck.

Naturally, she viewed him differently at breakfast. She had

risen earlier, although not exactly deliberately to arrive at the same time as his family, since she was awake anyway. But they came down simultaneously into the fresh dining room. The boy looked across at her intently, almost as if aware that he had kept her company that night, and she realized that in an establishment like this, any change of habit was instantly noticeable.

She walked down to the beach. She was really quite passably tanned now, despite that one overcast day. She could mingle into the holiday crowds without standing out as a newly arrived northerner. She enjoyed watching Italian paterfamilias glance casually at the pleasing contrast between her shoulders and the blue straps of her sundress. Her age lines showed up as little white arrows when she stopped smiling.

Her attitude to the Villa Olga softened. It did its best to keep up an appearance of postcard serenity but it could never totally succeed. Not even that blandness and soothing routine could keep the unpredictable at bay. She greeted the drilling as a reminder of the invigorating outside world.

On the beach, she heard his brother call him Luigi. She was quite dismayed for in her mind he had been first nameless, an entertaining, mythological idea, and then possibly Giulio or Guido. In the afternoon, Luigi's family set out on an excursion. They left after lunch, with thermos flasks and maps, and Cordelia lay in her room, imagining their fractious expedition. She felt slightly weary after her disturbed night and eventually closed the shutters for a siesta. Through her thin afternoon sleep, she was aware of her imagination continuing, pleasurably preparing the next development. In one dream, Luigi was carried back from the expedition with a sprained ankle, minute droplets of perspiration caught in the light hairs of his lip. She comforted him. In another, she was confronted by a picture which embarrassed her as soon as she awoke of herself and Luigi frolicking wholesomely in the waves like a resort advertisement.

When she got up, she felt the need to walk and chose the further ice-cream parlour as a goal. It embodied the sugary existence of the Villa Olga but it did so with a more calculated grace. She walked along the seafront, benign after sleep, and took a white chair under the awning. Here, she would treat Luigi to a mammoth sundae, surreptitiously watching the ice-cream form a milky wave on his upper lip. She ordered a coffee. Around her, families were making a tremendous business of choosing between the complex flavours. When she saw Luigi, his arrival was so much in keeping with her thoughts that, for a few seconds, she did not remember that there was a reason why he should not be there; he had set out on an excursion with his family at two o'clock and they were not due to return till dinner. For a fantastic moment, Cordelia felt she might be responsible. The boy saw her as well, so it seemed natural to beckon him to come over and share her table. She greeted him with polite astonishment.

"Why are you back so early?"

He flushed and then set his head defiantly. "I said I had a headache. At the bus garage, suddenly, I could not stand the prospect of going with all of them to Santa Cecilia and the fuss about seats and Papa reading aloud from the guidebook so I turned round and came back." He looked at her to see if she would give him away.

"Well, let me treat you to an ice-cream." That, surely, showed her trustworthiness.

Abruptly, he declined, "I have money."

Cordelia noted how young he was. "Well, yes, I'm sure you have, but why not save it? Let me."

The waiter was at hand. She turned and asked for another coffee and then gestured to the boy. He ordered an ice-cream a little unwillingly and then sat for a minute and looked moodily out to sea. Cordelia was conscience-stricken. Perhaps, for him, choosing an ice-cream was intimate, might reveal more than he wanted to about himself. Instead of bossily insisting, she should have let him go inside with the waiter and make his selection in private. Whether inhibited by her presence, his choice was impeccable, nothing too infantile, nothing pink; coffee, pistachio, grand marnier. He thanked her formally when it was brought and began to eat it solemnly.

"You're not having any?"

Cordelia shook her head. "Coffee's all I want."

He nodded. "That's probably why you keep a figure, unlike Mama."

The compliment was quite devastated by the comparison. Of course, of course, he must put her in the same category as his mother, but his unquestioning bluntness was still disappointing.

"Thank you."

He looked up at the facetious tone of her voice, considered her wry expression and looked back at the ice-cream, which posed less problems. He felt under an obligation to provide conversation in payment for it. "Where do you come from?"

Cordelia told him and he nodded, but said nothing. She had no idea what he knew of London. She had a quick vision of him as one of the crowd of foreign youngsters squatting around the Eros statue at Piccadilly Circus. He had that capacity for hunched resentment.

"And your husband?" he asked. "What does he do?"

"I'm not married," Cordelia said. It was her turn now to worry he would give her away; spread the word of her footloose condition through the boarding house and cause everyone's manner to her primly to change.

He pretended to be more absorbed than he was in his ice-cream. To help him out of his embarrassment, Cordelia pointed into the dish, "Look, the same colours as the Villa Olga and the Villa Roma and Sans Souci," the two boarding houses on either side.

He wrinkled up his nose. "Don't put me off." In a spontaneous game, he added, "If you had to allot everyone there a flavour, what would it be?"

They giggled.

171

"Oh, strawberry for Signora Amelia," said Cordelia, with a ridiculous vision of her two great, mammary scoops. "And liquorice obviously for the Padre."

"Bombe Surprise for my father," said Luigi. Then he did something she was sure no English boy of his age would have thought of. He said, "And I think pistachio for you," and helped himself to an insolent, lingering spoonful.

That night, she wondered, why pistachio; her oddity, her envy, her green eyes? Luigi's father unexpectedly wished her good evening on the way in to dinner and she was momentarily alarmed by the idea that Luigi might have spoken to him about her. She would find herself cast as a prowling baby-snatcher. But it was so unlikely that he would have. Luigi himself did not appear at dinner, presumably still keeping up the pretence of feeling unwell. She felt glad she had bought him the ice-cream.

The drilling interrupted a terrible dream in which one of the exhibits for which she was responsible in the Arnold Teller Gallery had disappeared, and the main body of suspects was a party of Italian schoolchildren, who were being shown round when the object was stolen. The prime suspect was Luigi, who was being interrogated with uncharacteristic violence by Mr Waite and Jonathan and Cyril. He would reveal nothing, but stood bravely unflinching under their cries, a look of anguish on his brown face.

She was relieved to see him at breakfast; yesterday's episode was over. She waited for him to appear on the beach. She intended to give him one of her books. After some time, she realized he was again sitting a short way off, apparently waiting to be invited, but no nearer than on her second day. Unreasonably exasperated, she sat up and called him. How early a child learns what is male behaviour in this country, she thought, approaching just enough to involve her, but not enough to become embroiled. But Luigi barely looked at her. It was only when she threatened to call again and the sound of her English voice would have drawn attention from the beach that he stood up and came over. But he did not sit down beside her.

"Allora," she said coquettishly, "did they guess?"

"My parents are not over-endowed," he said woodenly.

Cordelia patted the sand beside her. "Make yourself at home."

"No thank you."

It wasn't easy talking up at Luigi from the sand with the sun shining right behind his head.

"You went hungry last night."

He sighed gustily at such an obvious statement.

"Have your parents asked you who this funny lady is you keep talking to?"

Luigi bore down into the sand with his foot in embarrassment. What is the matter with me, thought Cordelia, why am I behaving like this?

He drilled quite a hole with his toes before he answered, "My father asked, naturally. He would."

"I hope you had nice things to say about me."

The boy looked down at her in sudden fierce disgust. "Why should I?" he said desperately, "I hate that sort of thing. It's so vulgar."

Cordelia wanted to find the book for Luigi in her beach bag. As she started to look for it, he took advantage of her averted face to blurt, "By the way, thank you for the ice-cream yesterday," and when she looked up to dismiss his thanks lightheartedly, he gave her a stern nod and walked primly away.

Luigi's father wished her good day again at lunch. He stood back ostentatiously to allow her first into the dining room. Luigi's mother did not wish her good day.

In the afternoon, she went to bed, as much to escape from Miramare as to rest. The gap between her holiday and her imagination had stretched to breaking point. She had written on the flyleaf of her book "For Luigi, in memory of Miramare, Summer 81", and it lay rejected, no, not even offered, on her bedside table. She organized a dream in which Cyril at first wryly watched her carryings on while he smoked a great cigar and later merged rather disturbingly with his cigar smoke.

Luigi's mother was not at dinner, a likely sign of further family discord. It was said she had a migraine and the landlady was full of tutting and offers of broth. Cordelia lingered over her dinner, faintly intrigued, in the hope that Luigi might, somehow or other, convey the true story to her. She even ordered one of the house desserts, which she had so far ignored, and the landlady rapturously brought her a big slab of almond pudding and stood by her while she ate it. When she could protract her meal no longer, she went through on to the veranda. Someone followed her out shortly. She half turned, hoping for Luigi, but it was his father, preening his moustache in pleasurable anticipation.

She spent the last day avoiding him. He tramped the length of the beach in uncharacteristic exertion until he found her and then plumped himself down beside her with a compliment on her suntan. He scolded the landlady for maybe keeping Cordelia waiting with her lunch. Worst of all, he insisted on speaking English to her, weighty, pedantic utterances, the laboriously acquired speech of a late learner. Of Luigi, there was no sign. Presumably he had left the two of them, Cordelia and his father, to their vile ways and was now sitting by himself somewhere, reinforced in his adolescent condemnation of the adult world. He did not look at Cordelia during dinner but his father toyed meaningfully with his repulsive moustache. She went up early and packed with little nostalgia. Her last night at the Villa Olga, she did not dream.

On the morning of September the seventh, she woke in expectation of the drilling for the last time. It was Sunday. She pushed open her shutters and looked out across the tidy street to the sea. The beach was pale and blank and empty. Tomorrow, she would be back in her wintry room at the museum, imagining that, drawn by her suntan, Cyril had come back to her.

The Other Launderette

Going to the launderette in the Place des Innocents was almost
fun. I had switched my allegiance from a grubby little
six-machine establishment at the end of the street when I found
out that at the Place des Innocents there were nearly current
issues of *Paris Match* and *Jours de France* and the woman who
minded the washing machines was svelte and soignée. The
caretaker at the other launderette was, I am afraid to say, a
most gruesome hag. No, not a hag, maybe; more a harpy, for
she exuded a definitely lewd quality, despite her hideous
appearance. A mat of dark, long hair flapped around her bloated
face. She had mottled, swollen cheeks, which she sucked in and
out obsessively. Her eyes flickered under thick, raw lids, which
you could imagine being sold by weight in a charcuterie. She
wore consistently a giant brown knitted cardigan over an old,
flowery dress and, possibly most horribly of all, a pair of
grubby, flirtatious little slippers, which seemed a mockery of
her distended feet.

She called me, "Meestur". My first visit to the launderette
ought really to have been my last. But, in a silly way, one
relishes these sordid experiences abroad, which one would not
tolerate at home. I came in with my great bag of dirty washing
and my accent, as I asked for a cup of detergent, informed her
straight away that she had an Englishman on her hands. "Ah
Meestur," she cried warmly, bustling forward. She sized up my
recent haircut and reasonably good jacket and then waddled
into her cubby-hole at the back to fetch the detergent. She stood
over me as I loaded a machine, perhaps intentionally the one

175

nearest the door, and seemed full of curiosity about my clothes. I was rather embarrassed. I had spent most of the last month settling down in the city and certainly hadn't given much thought before then to washing my clothes. They were pretty distasteful. But the caretaker did not seem concerned by all the grey collars and dubious socks. She bent forward and examined them frankly. "What kind of collars are those?" she asked. "That pullover, is it Shetland?" I bundled my things in as fast as I could and tried to hide the underpants inside the shirts. But my reticence did not discourage her and in her eagerness to see properly, she craned even closer. Then I noticed that she was none too fresh herself.

I sat down to wait and opened my book. Behind me, the caretaker had a mystifying conversation with another customer about her life. "There are days", I heard her say in an addled voice, "when I wonder how I cope with it all, really I do. It's more than a normal person can bear. What with Their foreign coins jamming up the machines and flooding and now a whole house of Them opposite to cap it all, sometimes, honestly, I just wish it would end."

When my machine finished, she was at the ready, with a plastic basket to transfer the clothes to a dryer. I took it from her rather promptly and protested, "Non, non, madame, let me." I tried to imply that I was doing it out of politeness but, of course, it was to avoid her fingers pawing my clothes. She beamed all over at being treated with such respect.

I cannot remember exactly when I came back for the second time. I am not all that keen on washing so let's say it was three or four weeks later. It would have been in the evening because the place was very full and I remember feeling relieved that the caretaker's attentions would be generally shared. The other customers were mainly Arabs, skinny, moustached labourers, staring mournfully at the turning drums. The air was blue with cheap cigarette smoke. The harpy was behaving atrociously. Through the steam and cigarette smoke, she was bellowing, apparently at no one in particular, "Vile, that's what it is, vile. Maybe it's all right to carry on like that in some countries, but don't you dare try it here." I couldn't quite understand what the matter was, but I assumed that someone had unhygienically broken some regulation of the launderette.

The woman was quite immense in her fury. Every now and then, she would make an angry rush at one of the small men and almost jostle him, crying, "Oh yes, go on, sit there, pretend it's nothing to do with you. You don't fool me, Mohammed, I know you're all the same."

I put my clothes in as fast as possible and went out to walk around the evening. When I came back about half an hour later, the launderette had cleared and the caretaker's rage seemed to have focused on one man. He was sitting rigidly straight at the end of the bench, self-righteously watching his clothes bump round and round in the suds, while, above him, the crazed figure hissed and squawked. She turned to me as I came in and cried, "Ah, Meestur, tell this wretch how gentlemen behave in your country. They have such filthy habits where he comes from." The Arab barely moved his head in my direction. He had clearly decided to submit to this persecution in silence, for the sake of clean clothes. I admired his tenacity.

"It's cold outside, isn't it?" I said rather feebly and burrowed into the dank drum to extract my washing. Behind me, the enraged caretaker gave a harsh laugh.

Then I came again in the daytime, on my day off. I had a newspaper, which I intended to hold up in front of my face, if necessary, like a screen. But the place was shut. An impromptu paper notice on the door said "Closed Hour Due Circumstances". I was walking back down the street, feeling displeased, when I heard a shriek behind me. I turned round to see the launderette woman, arms flailing extravagantly, beckoning to me from a café doorway. She called, "It's all right Meestur. We're opening right away. It's fine for you." I hesitated. She darted back into the café and reappeared with a half-full glass of porto. She bobbed it at me explanatorily and then patted her cardigan pocket where, presumably, she kept her keys. Oh well, I thought limply, I'll get the chore over with. I started to go reluctantly back towards the launderette; I did not relish the prospect of half an hour's intimacy with the harpy. When I reached the café doorway, she cackled placatingly and, to my dismay, actually suggested I came in for a drink too. "I'm in a hurry," I said rather brusquely, "I haven't got time." "Ah bon, ah bon," the woman said good-humouredly and, causing me slight guilt, she downed her glass, returned it to the bar and came hobbling up the street with me to her launderette.

That time, I came close to abandoning the horrid place. In the steamy gloom—she did not bother to switch on all the lights just for me—there was a melancholic atmosphere, which provoked the miserable woman to confide in me. (Was that glass of porto her first?) She sat down beside me on the long bench and, for a minute, just watched my clothes turn sympathetically, as if they were whimsical fish frolicking in an aquarium. "They're pretty, aren't they?" she said, "all those sleeves hugging each other."

"Well now, I'd better do my shopping," I said and she placed her hand, briefly, on my knee.

"You cook for yourself, do you?" she asked tenderly. "Dinner for one?"

My life in the city had never struck me as pathetic till then; I rather enjoyed the ritual of cooking on my single gas ring, going down to the market to choose fruit and cheese. But there was something so ghastly behind her maudlin enquiry that I suddenly felt desperate. I had a vision of myself eating a meal on my own, all off the one plate, with a book in front of me, that horrified me by its nightmarish solitude.

"It's not always easy on one's own, is it?" she went on, "I know all about it, believe me. I've been through it all since my husband died."

"Yes," I said, standing up, "I have to buy some dinner." I added brutally, "I've invited friends."

I came back half an hour later with a loaded bag of groceries. I had missed the moment to unload my clothes and they were already rotating in the dryer. The caretaker welcomed me back with approval. "You're a good boy," she said primly, "you keep your clothes nice and clean, I see."

I blenched, but she did not seem inclined to continue the theme. She was smoking, with one elbow propped on a washing-machine, and she appeared uncharacteristically placid. I topped up the dryer with one-franc pieces and opened my paper. Behind me, the woman stubbed out her cigarette with a nasty grinding noise and began on some launderette job. There was a fair bit of dragging and sighing, which I resolutely ignored. Then she appeared momentously in front of me with an armful of dirty washing. "You keep your clothes nice and clean," she repeated, unfolding her bundle, "Not like some people." And, to my utter disgust, she started to display the inner crevices of the clothes, dismally encrusted with filth and grime. "Sickening," she said. "Isn't it? Vile."

I could only stammer, "Who—whose are they?"

She swelled triumphantly as she said, "Theirs. They're all as bad as each other when it comes to cleanliness, you know, those Arabs."

After this, needless to say, I more than dreaded the place. I did go again, once or twice, before the dénouement, but nothing memorable happened. Visits to the launderette hardly constitute events in the normal course of affairs. I was leading a full, rich life in the city and I certainly didn't look to the launderette for any sleazy thrill.

Then, about six months ago, I went there for the last time. The woman wasn't in the launderette, but the door was open when I arrived so I went in and put my clothes in to wash. It was a relief to find the place empty. I sat down in front of my machine, lit a cigarette and stretched my legs. After maybe ten minutes, I noticed a lopsided couple approaching along the opposite side of the street; a teetering female balloon and a

179

minute male. It was not until they were nearly opposite and turning to cross the road that I actually registered what my vision held. It was the caretaker, arm in arm with one of the Arabs. I stayed rooted to the bench, unable to react for surprise and shock. They crossed the street and came up to the door of the launderette. To my amazement, I recognized the little man whom the harpy had abused so viciously in the launderette that night a few months previously. They came in cosily and we said "Bonjour." The woman looked pink and very pleased with herself, her little slippers clopped on the tiles. I had stood up, expecting some sort of confrontation, but she seemed quite unembarrassed by my presence.

"Bonjour Meestur," she trilled, "All O.K. with the machine? No problems?" The Arab eyed me sullenly and I answered brightly, "Oh no, oh no. I think it's almost finished." They went through into the little cubby-hole at the back and then the woman came out again with a scrap of paper in her hand. She grinned at me unspeakably and up went that tatty sign again, "Closed Hour Due Circumstances".

I hurried to finish. I was overcome with such revulsion for the place, I could hardly wait to leave it. I was a naïve idiot, I told myself; if ever there was a den of vice, this was it. The caretaker treated me like a regular. She padded cosily around her establishment, letting down the Venetian blinds, turning out the lights, until I felt I was becoming involved in their foul act. She even asked me to join them for an aperitif.

I banged the glass door behind me and, having found a better launderette, I never went back. There had been preliminary giggles from the cubby-hole as I fumed in front of the dryer and, twice, the small Arab had come out and glared at me.

I felt resentful. That revelation had shown me that, in certain respects, I was still a callow English public schoolboy, with stale socks. I loathed the place which had proved it and, in what is, I suppose, a classic act of revenge, I decided to write about it. In time, my indignation was moderated by pity. What a wretched, debased world they inhabited.

The smart supervisor and the magazines at the Place des Innocents were all very fine. But I could not help feeling sometimes, as I sat under the blown-up photographs of Alpine meadows, that I was dodging the issue by coming here and that the other launderette was real life.

Robert Sproat

Stunning the Punters
Like Some Royal King of Honour all upon the
Banks of Troy
Question Marks

Stunning the Punters

It's a rough old estate. Be about that time when me and Spike—this whole thing I'm telling you about was his idea really, but we'll get to that in a minute—we'd just come out the entrance of our block; we was hanging about on the front steps arguing the toss about where to go and *wham*, there's this really terrific fucking crash right behind us. Know what it was? Only a pram. Right, a real old-fashioned metal pram, with the big wheels and the spring suspension and everything, smashed to fucking bits. "Fuckers must have pushed it off the roof," says Spike, "far too fucking big to go through them windows." Fourteen floors, straight down. "Ten points," I says to Spike, "got to be a maximum." "Nah," says Spike "only get a maximum for a pram if the baby's still in it." As it happens, that was about the last real pram I ever seen. All them collapsibles and these back-to-front papoose things nowadays, isn't it, with the baby bouncing about getting suffocated in its mother's tits. Expect you'd only get a maximum for one of them if the mother was still wearing it.

Spike's the one who should be telling you all this, Jack the lad, old Spike, but that's impossible the way things turned out, isn't it? Still, you'll be all right with me, got a good memory, I have. Only one out of the lot of us got any O-levels, and that was just from remembering a lot of stupid stuff without really trying. I used to listen to people talking and practise remembering what they said, you know. You ever do that? Really listen to what people say, when they're talking to each other, not to you, I mean? I used to do it because I like to imitate

185

people, take the piss out of them, used to make old Spike cry laughing, I did. And I'll tell you one thing I noticed, you can't take the mickey properly unless first of all you got them down exact, all the details. Perhaps if you had a memory as good as mine you wouldn't need to hump that cassette thing around with you. People really do say amazing fucking things to each other, though. Like, there was these two drunks in here a couple of weeks ago, middle-aged geezers in good suits, and one of them was at the stage where he can't be told nothing, and he keeps saying, "I don't give a trot. Not a *trot*." And a bit later on, they're ripping some other geezer to shreds, and the same one says, "He doesn't know his arse from tuppence." Then again, coming home tonight on top of the 41 through Crouch End, this old couple was sitting in front, pair of fatties, him in an Andy Capp and she looks like someone's Gran. The thing I noticed was, whatever he says, she just nods and goes, "Hm hm hm hm hm." Five times, always exactly five times. Most of what he's saying is dead boring, hang the lot of them, price of fags, bleeding unions, and I'm just thinking about joining in the next Hm hm hm hm hm bit, but all of a sudden, in the exact same tone of voice and everything, he goes, "I wish I was more like Jesus Christ so's I'd be less like Judas Iscariot." "Hm hm hm hm hm." Not a flicker, she's heard it a million times. "Course, there's electricity all around us," he says, "in the air, and through your bones and brains and blood and everything." "Hm hm hm hm hm." Nine points, I thinks, and a maximum if they keep it up till the Hale, but they got off just past the Black Boy in West Green Road.

To get back to what you was asking about, I still reckon it was really them that started it. The blacks, I mean. We got on all right with them for years, didn't we? I mean, we used to call them samboes and they used to call us honkies, but it was all a laugh, nothing meant. Oh, our old man was always going on about blackies this, Pakis that, but we never paid him no mind any more than we did over anything else. The Beer-gut That

Stunning the Punters

Walks Like A Man, Kenny used to call him. But there was never anything really nasty between us and the blacks as far as the kids was concerned. I mean, half the faces on the North Bank was black. At least. And when me and Spike and Alf Rabaiotti got nicked the day we took Millwall, Piggy Mackintosh got nicked right alongside us, and Piggy's as black as Newgate's knocker. When the punks first started and they was rolling into school with the green and pink hair and that, the blacks was on the same side as us skins, you know. Actually used to join in and help us kick shit out of the stupid fucking wimps. They was normal, then, just like us, loved a good ruck. That's another thing that gets me, when people on the telly and that are going on about riots and rucks and things, and they're trying to tell you kids do that stuff because of unemployment, got no valid means of self-fulfilment, alienated from adult society and all that *New Society* shit they used to push at us in Social Studies. That's a load of fucking bollocks. You don't do it because of that. You do it because it's *fun*. How can you be so stupid that you can't twig that? Anyway, I reckon it was the blacks who cut themselves off from the rest of us in the first place, at least as far as the kids was concerned. It was that Rasta shit done it. You know, the dreadlocks and the stripey woollen hats and the Hai-Jai-Rastafari and the stupid fucking chug-a-lug-a-Babylon music. All of a sudden, the blacks are all off in their own special bit of the playground, and most of them won't even speak to whitey, them as ain't too spliffed to speak at all. It's like making out we hate them somehow makes them feel more important or something. Like when little kids create because they'd rather get belted by Mum than ignored, maybe. I think what really brought it home was Piggy Mackintosh. Piggy Mackintosh was born next door to me, shut your eyes when he's speaking and you wouldn't know what colour his face was. But one day I'm walking down by Bruce Grove station and Piggy comes up and goes, "Wot de raarss time, mon, mi fokkin bitch watch losting tree minutes a hour."

187

Anyway, after a bit, Spike says, "Fuck this, I'm going to join the National Front." I tells him he's only doing it to take the piss out of his old man, and I still think that's the truth. Spike's a yid, isn't he? I mean a real yid, a Jewish one, or at least a lapsed Jewish one, not some stupid fucking wally from Tottenham Supporters' Club. His old man sells kosher butchery and stuff down Stamford Hill, and he's got the full rig, black hat, whiskers, the lot. And Spike's always taking the piss out of him, like telling him he's turning vegetarian but not to worry, Dad, going to insist on ritually slaughtered vegetables. And when he first got the skinhead cut, he tells him it's because all his life he's wanted to hear someone say to him, that's funny, you don't look Jewish. Truth is, even before the skinhead hairdo, Spike looks about as Jewish as Bjorn Borg.

But Spike insists he's serious, and he starts bringing NF mags and stuff to school and flyposting and that. And pretty soon he's got Alf Rabaiotti and Denny Plumb and Barry Crump and one or two of the other skins to join the Front, but not me. I don't believe in joining things, do I? But I still knock around with the lads, same as usual. And I don't know what sort of stuff they're pumping into Spike and the rest down the NF, but it seems to me like Spike's getting some sort of Great British Hero complex or something. He's saying stuff like we got to stop all this talk about how we ain't real hard skins like the old days, people saying there ain't been a proper skinhead since Slade let their hair grow, saying we're just a bunch of wimps with short haircuts talking hard to each other to forget how scared we really are. And he's saying there's no class in having rucks with wallies like punks and mods, what we got to concentrate on is getting stuck into the jigaboos. All this is happening just as we're finishing our last year at school, by the way. Most of us just bunked off after the exams were finished, and Alf Rabaiotti bunked off while they were still on. Alf's a tasty geezer in a bundle on account of being so fast and together and built like a rhino, but bright he ain't. But it gets to the point where Spike ain't satisfied with making life hard for the odd solo coon on the street, he's actually got us all going back to school for the sole purpose of having a go at them in strength. So there we all are, mob-handed, stomping along the playground in the old Doc Martens singing these anti-sambo songs Spike either made up or learnt down the NF, like Hit the Frog, Wog, and Haile Selassie's a Bonny Hielan' Lassie and they don't like it one bit. And we're giving them the old Blubberlips and Wanker signs, and in the end they rush us and there's one really terrific fucking ruck, grief and claret all over the shop. And they're real hard, some of them, but we're still really taking them apart when someone says the Old Bill's been called and we has to run for it. "Really good, what?" I says to Spike. "Nine points?" "Nah," he says, grinning all over his face, "no dead." And he's laughing and running at the same time, proper nutty-looking, all the wimps on the street getting out of his way like he's a runaway bus. And a funny thing strikes me while we're still running, but I don't tell Spike because I think it might go down wrong. What I'm thinking is, here's Spike and them going on about jungle bunnies and lower forms of life, animals and that, but the only way we was able to take them blacks was to go more animal than they could, how about that? And I'm starting to wonder how much of this race stuff the lads really believe in or is it just an excuse to go mad and have fun spreading grief, but it's best to keep shtum about that sort of thinking or someone's going to get the idea you're a *smart* sod, and *wallop*.

Off and on, we done that sort of caper most of that summer. Got ourselves barred from quite a few pubs and places, destroyed a few happy evenings at concerts and clubs and that. Spike and some of the rest were all tooled up to go on one of them big NF marches, but the law called it off at the last minute. I don't know about the other lads, but after a couple of months of it I'm secretly starting to find it all a bit tedious. Spike seems fidgety, too, and it's about this time he comes up with the stunt you was really asking about.

We was sitting in the boozer one night quite late, bored stiff, trying to come up with something to do that don't cost nothing, due to we're all borassic. Barry Crump says that last week the bouncer in that pub near the Angel Road Community Centre put Jimmy Tollington in hospital, so why don't we trundle over to Edmonton and send the sod on a long sickie, but you can see his heart ain't really in it. There's just the five of us, Barry, Spike, Alf Rabaiotti, Denny Plumb and me. Spike's acting like he's half asleep, but all of a sudden he perks up and starts getting ready to leave. "Come on, children," he says, "we're off to stun the punters." And he won't tell us where we're going or why, but we tag along because we know Spike and Spike seems to be fair bursting to get at whatever the great secret is. First off we need some transport, he tells us, and at that time we can probably scrape together two-thirds of a dead Honda 90 between the lot of us, so we have to nick a car. Sorry. Take it away and drive it without the owner's consent. "Denny," says Spike, "can you take away and drive without the owner's consent some wheels for us?" "Can a swim duck?" says Denny. "Any particular colour?" When Denny was nine, he got his picture in the paper for nicking a double-decker bus, one of them real old-fashioned RTs with no synchromesh or nothing, like you only see in the Transport Museum nowadays. Got it nearly half a mile down the road before he hit the law car, and that was only because he was too short to see over the bonnet and double-declutch at the same time. So in about ten minutes flat Denny takes away and drives without the owner's consent a nice inconspicuous Cortina Mark 3 from four streets away and brings it down the bus-stop where we're waiting for him. Spike tells him to drive it down towards Clapton and use the back doubles, but he still won't say exactly where we're going or why. Barry Crump says how about one point for every mod or punk we can make jump for it, two if we hit them and double points for niggers, but Spike says not, spoil the whole thing if we get nicked before we even get there. "There" turns out to be that big triangle of waste ground with railway lines on all three sides down the bottom end of the Walthamstow Marshes, where the line out of Liverpool Street divides just after it crosses the River Lea. Spike makes Denny drive right into the middle of the triangle and says we're leaving the motor there; even if it's reported missing, the Old Bill's never going to find it there before morning. Denny wants to nick the car radio but Spike says to leave it, we got work to do. "Come on," says Denny, "we're skint, that's a handsome radio, few quid there," but it's no use arguing with Spike when his mind's set on something, it's like trying to get money out of a bubble. "Follow me," says Spike. "Someone up there likes us tonight. Have one of you lot been being a good boy on the quiet?" And he explains how, like by magic, what we needs to do the job just happens to be kept right next to the ideal spot. All we got to do is break in and help ourselves. He's telling us all this while he's leading us along the towpath; it's a DIY warehouse we've got to get into, what we're after is paint. Under the railway bridge, Spike says "Hoo Hoo" to test the echo over the water, then "Abandon ship all ye who enter here!" "Do what?" says Alf Rabaiotti. "Morning, Alfred," says Spike, and tips Alf into the Lea. That's where we discover Alf can't swim, due to being the one person in three million or whatever with negative buoyancy, and Spike and Barry have to go in after him to stop him drowning. Everyone's laughing fit to bust by the time they gets him out, and Spike has a hard time getting us to listen while he explains he's got the ideal spot for slogan-painting, right by the main line, millions of punters going past on the train every day, all we need is paint. "Oh," says Alf Rabaiotti, "we going to do some painting?"

Well, Denny's in and out of the place in no time flat with jumbo aerosols for everybody, and we march out to where some factories and warehouses and things back on to the railway line. No worries about being seen from the trains; driver's watching the track, and you can't see nothing out a lighted coach when its dark outside, can you? Anyway, Spike says Alf has to have the honour of painting up the first slogan, which surprises me, because when it comes to stringing words together, Alf Rabaiotti is generally about as much use as a chocolate teapot. And I can't work out whether Spike's taking the piss or whether he's trying to make old Alf feel good after looking such a berk in the river. "Nice and big, now, Alf," says Spike. "They got to read it from the train," and Alf steps up and paints ABANDON WOGS SLUM. And there's a bit of a pause, like, and then Spike says, "Nice one," and suddenly everyone's clapping Alf on the back and punching him on the arm and he's got this great big grin on his stupid face. It comes to me clear, then, something I've only sort of half-noticed before, that Spike's got some kind of magic way of making people do what he wants, and making them do it good. "Last one to finish his spray-can's a wimp," says Spike, and we spread out along the track painting away like we was nutty or something. Well, you'd be surprised how much wall-space five blokes can fill up when they're racing each other, and when we're finished it's too long to read it all from any one spot, and it looks really good. None of the individual bits is all that great, but there's so fucking *much* of it. I notice everybody, me included, seems to have used ABAN-DON WOGS SLUM at least once, and I can see where old Alf's brains give up on him and he's lapsed into SPURS SHIT CHELSEA SHIT. "Ten points," says Spike. "Clear max-imum." Then we say goodnight and Spike goes off through the sidings to his place in the new estate on the other side of the line, and the rest of us come out through the playing-fields to see can we get a night bus back up here, due to Denny thinks two cars in one night might be pushing it.

And that's the last any of us ever saw of Spike. See, where we'd been was the British Rail track with the overhead electric, but them sidings is the marshalling-yard for London Transport, the Tube trains, with the old live rail. And we'll never know if old Spike slipped, or if he just plain forgot, but he was still pretty soaked from being in the Lea, so when he touched the live rail, *zap*.

Well, all the real devil seemed to go out of the lads after that. We gradually sort of drifted apart, like, especially after I got the driving job and the others are all still on the dole. Still see them on the street to say hallo to and that, but we're going around together less and less all the time. And though I've always got all the memories of old Spike lying around somewhere at the bottom of my mind, it's been maybe a year or more since I really thought much about any of it when I get sent on this delivery job out to Stansted airport. So I makes the drop, and I'm tooling along on my way home minding my own business, when this stupid fucking wally in a Morris Minor Traveller backs straight out of his weekend cottage garden on a blind corner and *smash*. He's got Nuclear Power No Thanks and Greenpeace and We have Eaten The Lions of Longleat stickers and all sorts of other shit all over his back windows, so I don't reckon he could have seen me even if he'd bothered to look. It's in absolutely perfect nick, or was till I hit it, and you can tell it's his pride and joy and he's probably even insured the no claims bonus and you know before he even gets out that he's about thirty-five and bald with baggy designer dungarees and a shoulder-bag. Oh what a terrible shame, I thinks, now you won't be able to pavement-park it in Camden Market (hey, that rhymes, maybe I could get a song together on that, eh?). But it turns out he's really nice about it, all his fault, sure you're OK, come in the house and have a cuppa while he phones for the breakdown wagon, because as well as killing the Morris, the smash has done my Transit no good whatsoever. And when the recovery truck geezer gets there, little fat smiley wop geezer, melon on legs, no neck, gold tooth, oily black hair, he just bends down and squints under the front end and starts making these No Way wop gestures with his arms straight down, like he was ruffling the heads of two little kids. "Ohohoho," he says, "Nononono," he says, "She ainta gonna fly no more," he says, and I have to get the train back from Bishop's Stortford.

193

When I get on the train, there's these two oldish geezers sitting facing each other at the table opposite, and they both look away very quickly after giving me angry little stares that tell me they're thinking, Please, God, make the nasty rough skinhead lout not sit near us, God. And straight away they start to talk to each other just a little bit louder, as if that, and not looking at me, is somehow going to magic me away. And it's a really *smart* conversation, making me think they're college professors from Cambridge or something. ". . . and as far as I can make him out, Lodge appears to be arguing that the structuralist approach is valid because it enables him to ensure that mediocre undergraduates can hand up more substantial and coherent essays." "Ha. Crap, absolute crap. Tail-wagging-dog-ism." But it don't bother me none, due to I've noticed when old people give you all them fierce frowns and that, it's really because they're frightened of you, not angry with you. So I just plonks my boots up on the seat opposite and gives this great big nutty smile which I know very well they can see out the corner of their eyes, and this makes them pretend even harder I'm not there. And they even start playing this college-professor game to keep the conversation from flagging ". . . you know the idea, the effects of the cuts are even spilling over into the titles of the stuff on the syllabus, Bleak Maisonnette, Moderate Expectations, that sort of thing." "Ha ha. You could have, um, Submicroscopic Dorrit," "Ha ha ha." And if the talk sounds a bit forced, you should hear the laughter. "The Grapes of Pique." "Ha ha ha." Funny how it's harder to make a meaningless noise like laughter sound real than it is to do the same with words. "John Halifax, Estate Agent." "Ha ha ha ha ha." Funny stuff, humour WELCOME TO WOGS SLUM Eh? What? FUCKING BLACK BARSTITS ABANDON TERRIBLE WOGS SLUM It's all there flashing past on the walls NIGGER BOY ANIMAL BURN WOG BABIES NOW But this ain't what we done, it's far too far north, way up near Brimsdown, miles away, we only done a hundred yards or so

ON FIRE SAMBO ABANDON WOGS SLUM TERRIBLE TERRIBLE it's grown, it's enormous, someone's been adding to it and adding to it, it's like it's going on for ever SHITHOUSE COONS OUT NOW Jesus Christ, it's *huge!* And the *hate* coming off those walls, it's got me flinching in case it knocks the train off the rails KILL WOG SHIT ABANDON TERRIBLE WOGS SLUM and it's kind of frightening to think something a bunch of brainless kids done for a stunt can grow into something this big, and I'm wondering if poor old Spike ever realized he could start something this *scarey*. And then I notice the professors is blind to it, still carrying on with their stupid game IF THEY'RE BLACK SEND THEM BACK "The Antepenultimate Mohican." "Ha ha ha ha ha." FUCKING BLACK BARSTITS "Oh, wait, wait, I think this one's a boss. The Life and Opinions of Tristam Lemonade." "Ha ha ha ha ha." TERRIBLE TERRIBLE ABANDON WOGS SLUM and then I suddenly twig that they know it's there, all right, they're regulars on the route, but they're ignoring it the exact same way they're ignoring me, because it scares the shit out of them and they don't want to see it. Them punters is well stunned, old Spike, I thinks, ten points, posthumous. SPURS SHIT CHELSEA SHIT ABANDON . . .

When we get past it all down by the Marshes, the poor old dead Cortina's still out there in the middle of the triangle of waste ground, and I'm wondering who got the radio.

Course, that's all ancient history now. Haven't seen any of the lads for ages. Heard Denny Plumb was in Brixton for breaking and entering, which don't surprise me, and someone was telling me the other day Barry Crump was getting married. Don't know what became of Alf Rabaiotti, but I bet he ain't married, probably still thinks what you do with girls is gob on their head off the top deck of a bus. And you can see I let my hair grow quite some time ago. What finally turned me, I seen this little kid about nine years old done out as a perfect miniature skin, haircut, boots, braces, the lot. Well, you can't go round looking like what a nine-year-old thinks is hard can you? Anyway, chances are nowadays the next skin you will see will have a telly-producer Dad in Parliament Hill Fields and think it's hard to write up shit like Tracey 4 Mark and Spliff + Snout in Finsbury Park and Camden Town and buy his boots in Kickself. I even seen one the other day with *green boots*.

But I was down that way again the other day, you know. Been down Petticoat Lane of a Sunday and decided to come home on the train for a change. And you know what? They cleaned it all off, wiped it out. The Council, or British Rail, or someone. Scrubbed it away, every word of it painted over where they had to. Must have taken ages, cost a small fortune. But I'll tell you something really queer. It felt worse going past there if anything. I mean, you can easily see where the writing's been, and you can't help thinking about all them geezers having to clean up all them walls and things that the train takes ages to get past even at top speed. And that immediately reminds you of what it used to say, and that it wasn't just you, lots of other people felt so bad about it they went to all this trouble to wipe it out. And the laugh is, all they done was make it worse. Because I can see other people on the train who more than likely do the journey every day, they're feeling it even more than me. See, they got no excuse not to look out the window now, but when they do, the marks of the clean-up sets their minds going, don't they? The scrubbed wall shouts out all that hate louder than the wiped-out writing did. Really strange, by pretending something's never been said, you can end up screaming it. You learn something every day.

ABANDON . . . (Tape ends here.)

Like Some Royal King of Honour all upon the Banks of Troy

Ganty Pugh lived in the derelict redbrick air-raid shelter at the foot of the Common Hills, about a hundred yards beyond the last houses as the road left the town going north. The town knew he was there all right, but that was about as much as it cared to know. Had you asked someone off-guard how long Ganty had been there, an unthinking "Dunno" or "Ever since I can remember" would have been the likeliest responses, even though most could have worked out the proper answer with a bit of thought. The town and Ganty were on the best of slightly distant terms with each other, but there was never any hint of friendship between them, still less intimacy. Their relations were very like those of polite neighbours in the pricier London dormitory suburbs. The town was none the less about as far from London as you could walk dry-shod due west, being near the tip of the snout on the pig's-head map of Wales.

Though the unfanciful town would probably have scoffed at the notion, it regarded Ganty in much the same way as it did the Sunderlands: not particularly pleasant, but hardly worth worrying over. The town had long since grown used to the old RAF flying-boats, by this time in the twilight of their service careers ten years after the end of the war. It rarely bothered to look up as they howled into and out of their base on the Haven. For the stranger, though, the first Sunderland was often sudden and stunning. The land at the shore of the estuary reared up steeply for a couple of hundred feet and the inland country was a series of low hills and haphazard shallow depressions. Out of

197

sight of the sea, the horizon was usually only a few minutes' walk away. The town's skewed and stretched grid of grey terraced streets covered the first two ridges inland and the hollow between them. In order to get down on to the sheltered water of the Haven at the right speed and angle, the flying-boats often crossed the town almost at rooftop height. The typical landing approach was from down a stiff and noisy wind, hidden by the skyline until the last moment unless you were at the very crest of a hill, unseen and unheard until the plane pounced into the sky at the chimney-tops, a roaring airborne Moby Dick, jut-jawed, barrel-bellied, as boorish and unlikely on the wing as a giant off-white pig. When this happened, locals had the disconcerting habit of stopping dead in their conversational tracks and resuming as though nothing had happened when talk became possible again, like sufferers from simultaneous attacks of *petit mal*. The older children had absorbed this practice and amplified it, making it a positive point of honour not to be disturbed by a plane, scorning as babyish any of their number forgetful enough to look skywards. The smaller ones, not wise enough as yet to wish themselves grown up, craned necks, screwed up eyes, stuck fingers in ears, prayed hard for the excitement of a crash, got none and grew up atheist, despite in the meantime attending as many as possible of the town's five Chapels in vain attempts to qualify for all five Sunday School Trips in one year.

Ganty Pugh, by contrast, never lost his first-timer's eyes and ears for the noisy old planes. He was regularly seen with his crumpled weasel-face straining upwards, gravity miraculously failing to pluck from the back of his grizzled head the battered once-white peaked cap which always looked vaguely nautical, despite having originally belonged to the milkman. Whenever the RAF were on exercises which entailed frequent take-offs and landings, the old man sat out among the furze and bracken above the Point, gazing dreamily at the Haven. "By buggered!" he would stage-whisper at each successful arrival or departure;

"By buggered!", thrusting his hands into the folds of the numberless overcoats that nobody cared to get close enough to count.

Ganty was like the Sunderlands in this respect: he was loud, but tolerated nevertheless to the point of being virtually ignored. He was a great talker, but no conversationalist. If you passed him on the road, he would always bawl out his reflex greeting, "Why-hi, boy!", regardless of which sex he addressed, "And bloody scummy old weather again too!", but he never stopped to chat. Despite this, Ganty's waking hours were an almost unbroken monologue, low incoherent rumbling grumblings punctuated by wild and deafening outbursts of bravura cursing. Like the stranger's first Sunderland, these could come as a bit of a shock. Early on a calm morning, you could be walking the narrow shingle beach below Hill Mountain a mile from the road and at peace with the world, but if Ganty Pugh happened to be patrolling the landward side of the hedge, your peace was always in danger of being shattered by a roar of "Captain Bastard Fuck!" (There was never much doubt about Ganty's capital letters.) When he wasn't talking, he sang. It was a penetrating sandpaper baritone, unsweet but bang in tune. Swelling and fading on the gusting southwesterlies of the pig's snout, it would inform farm-workers half a field away that Holland was a wonder place and therein grew fine green. "Hiya, Ganty!" they would yell when he appeared at a gap in the hedge. "Why-hi, boy! And bloody scummy old . . ." More often than not, the bloody scummy old weather would whip away the tail of the greeting. Whether singing or cursing, the voice, like the uncounted overcoats, was several sizes too large for its owner. Ganty Pugh was a natural featherweight who had shrivelled rather than thickened with age. The voice belonged to a giant.

Sergeant Waldo Persimmon Walters never used the middle name foisted on him by his fat foolish Mam, although in his blacker moments he believed that the rest of the town, and especially his constables, did so out of his hearing. Waldo's moments were seldom black, however, since he had, in some way which always struck him as both mysterious and hilarious, managed to end up doing for pay the one job he would gladly have paid to do. The Royal Welch discipline ingrained in him during the war enabled him to run, in his reasonably humble opinion, as near perfect a four-man police station as you could hope to find, and if he did things by the book, large sections of that book were of his own authorship. New constables quickly ran up against Waldo's fanatical refusal to let a single charge of resisting arrest or assaulting the police sully the records of his station. "What's the matter with you?" he would demand to know. "Can't you even bloody look after yourself? I need coppers, not cry-baby bloody nancy-boys." Magistrates' Court officials, too, had over the years come to relish those occasions when Waldo gave evidence before Gomer Jenkins, JP, and were unfailingly fascinated by the sergeant's ability to maintain impeccable respect for the court while doggedly and democratically refusing to call his grocer his worship. In the book that Sergeant Walters had written to do things by, Ganty Pugh was clearly and unalterably down as Not a Matter For the Police.

Nobody but Bertha Price would ever have thought of trying to change that entry in Waldo's book and, as the town said when it heard, thought didn't enter into it in Bertha's case. Temper, malice, pride, will, aggressive respectability as resistible as a steam-roller? Certainly. Thought? Never. Bertha talked nearly as much as Ganty Pugh, not half as loud but twice as fast, and most of the time she was telling someone else what to do. She was already in full flight when she swept into the station, and all Waldo could catch of her opening sally was ". . . something got to be done, Sergeant, *got* to be," whereupon Bertha was forced to pause for breath. "Mrs Price, Mrs Price, calm down please, no point in upsetting yourself, ruin your dinner," Waldo said. Constable John Hughes entered from the rest room, surveyed the scene briefly, tipped his helmet to Mrs Alderman Price and turned his poker face to the task of readying his bicycle for the road. Bertha was away again at breakneck pace, ". . . was coming along the Prom, I always walk round that way for the air except when it's wet, and then I generally just ring through to the shop and ask them to deliver, so convenient, the phone I mean, and I could see him down on the beach and I always think he looks like he's up to no good, the way he stares at you with his eyes, and when I come up level with him he was down by the boathouse slip, and he was rooting about in all that old filth and seaweed and stuff, and he was roaring away, cursing and swearing, filthy old language, I have never been so black affronted, he said Eff, and it's not *decent*, it is utterly *beyond*, and something got to be done, Sergeant, *got* to be. . . ." Waldo had meanwhile calmly taken his fountain pen from his pocket, unscrewed the cap, placed it firmly on the other end of the pen's body and positioned himself to write. He radiated serene and reasonable patience in Bertha's direction. "Who?" he asked mildly. "That, that, that, that, that *creature*, that Ganty Pugh!" Bertha said. "Captain Bastard Hell," John Hughes said quietly through his teeth. "What?" said Mrs Alderman Price. "Well, well, well," said Constable Hughes. Waldo had put the cap back on his pen and clipped it into his pocket again. "Mrs Price," he said firmly, "Ganty Pugh is entirely harmless. You have my personal assurance. I have made a point of checking it personally. He harms nobody. He doesn't steal, he doesn't beg, he doesn't fight, he doesn't damage people's property, he doesn't drink hardly, only when he's got a few bob after potato-picking and then he's no trouble. Unlike Some." (Bertha had good reason to blush at this point if not the grace to. As it was, she managed, most uncharacteristically, not to interrupt Waldo's lecture. She was almost certain that Waldo had saved her from abject humiliation when Alderman Sidney Price had been among the illegal drinkers in the Admiral's Club while the police, in one of their periodic gestures of appeasement towards the Chapel lobby, had raided it at one in the morning. Showing surprising presence of mind for a man on the outside of ten pints

201

of HB, Sidney had slipped out through the French windows and climbed up an apple tree. Unfortunately, a uniformed constable had immediately stationed himself just beside that very tree, and Alderman Price eventually undid all his own good work by falling both asleep and out of the tree, breaking his thigh, beshitting himself and arriving in hospital with dirty underpants. Of course, the town knew all about this, the town *always* knew, but no charges had been brought, nothing had come out in court, nothing had got into the paper.) "And if he was swearing, Mrs Price, I'm sure he wasn't swearing at you, was he? Ganty Pugh don't talk to nobody, really, only himself, and if he is a bit loud, I can't arrest a man for having a loud voice. And if I *was* to lock up everyone in this town who swears, I wouldn't be able to move for prisoners. Only the four cells I got and I expect I could've filled the whole County Jail already this morning, and it's only quarter to eleven." Bertha dimly suspected the unchangeability of the Pugh entry in Waldo's book, but she was not equipped for graceful backing down. She didn't necessarily mean arrest him, she protested, but couldn't the sergeant sort of, well, have a word with him? Waldo, however, was well aware that Bertha would never be able to admit even to her respectable self what she meant by that: that Waldo should privately offer Ganty the choice of a bloody good hiding or mending his ways. "Have a word with him, Mrs Price?" Waldo asked. "Have a word with him? Ganty Pugh haven't shown no sign of understanding a single word said to him since before the old king died. The man is doolally, Mrs Price. Doolally tap." Ungracefully, Bertha backed down. John Hughes whistled the national anthem as she swept out.

Neither the town nor Ganty appeared to pay much heed to events in the world at large. The town's attention was firmly focused on more important local matters; Ganty gave little sign of having much attention to focus on anything abstract. In the world at large, restless natives were taking to slaughtering British expatriates as a short-lived empire faded faster than the pink on the school-atlas pages. Shocking, said the town, and did you see where they put Ernie Lloyd back in Carmarthen for interfering with them two little girls? (Sexomaniac he is, you know, his mental's fine, it's the sex.)

"*O love is pleasing and love is teasing, and love is a joy when first it's new,*" sang Ganty Pugh.

Suez finished Mr Eden, Russia marched into Hungary, and NATO exercises filled the Haven with Yankee ships. The town roused itself briefly, but lost interest after the USN Shore Patrols billy-clubbed into insensibility any American rating who even looked like doing something worth talking about. Shocking, said the town, and is it true about Arnold Perkins and his sister?

"*Way, hey, roll and go!*" sang Ganty.

A cautious provincial year or so behind the world at large, the town's older children became teenagers and rocked and rolled. The town bridled, smirked and continued to know best. Every year, bristling with the monoglot chauvinism of Little England Beyond Wales and unaware of the Dyfed to come, the Urban District Council solemnly recorded its refusal to levy a rate in support of the Welsh-only National Eisteddfod. Quite right too, said the town in a Welsh accent. Every few months, Denmark Arthur succumbed to nostalgia and ran up the Danish flag in the front garden of his council house. Every time, Sergeant Walters was called for and Denmark Arthur suddenly lost all command of the English language, watching in sullen silence as his flag was hauled down. Quite right too, said the town, couldn't have that, it's Foreign, and against Council regulations.

"*There's no fame and gold, only rain and cold, in this bitter foreign land,*" sang Ganty Pugh.

In Front Street, Tommy Pete Morris celebrated three continuous years of trying to find a job by losing his mind, setting fire to the front room and stoning his wife and children as they fled in the direction of the in-laws. Late that evening, he appeared in the garden with a shot-gun, discharged both barrels at his wife through a closed window and took to the fields, clearly believing himself a murderer. His wife escaped with minor cuts, but Waldo Walters nevertheless sent for reinforcements and tracker dogs from County HQ. Three days later, Tommy Pete was cornered in a ploughed field nine miles upriver. The inspector raised the loud-hailer to tell him his wife was alive and well. Before he could speak, Tommy Pete put the muzzle in his own mouth and blew the top of his head off. At least he done that bit right, said the town.

"If I didn't have had my sewing machine I'd have come to no good end," sang Ganty Pugh.

On ninety-nine days out of a hundred, nothing so dramatic happened, but the town continued to live, to age, to change. Chimney-stacks sprouted TV aerials. People bought washing-machines, then fridges or even cars. Dr Beeching closed the railway station. The RAF pensioned off the Sunderlands. Nice to have a bit of peace and quiet, said the town, and have you seen the price of coal?

"Captain Bastard Bugger!" mourned Ganty Pugh, "Captain Bastard *Bastard!*"

Ninety-nine out of a hundred of Sergeant Walters' working days were spent recording petty pilfering, locking up drunks for the night, charging the town's new motorists with parking without lights, doing the paperwork for unexplained deaths, deciding when to intervene in the wordless grim-faced fist-fights that broke out after closing time, destroying unwanted dogs with his Webley service revolver at the bottoms of back gardens. People continued to get born, grow up, get married, die. Chapel attendances dwindled towards single figures. The cinema closed. In ten years, four men hanged themselves from four separate sets of banisters. Another decade had slipped under the town's guard. The world at large had changed, and the town was less inclined to regard the world at large as Somewhere Else.

"O indeed I have, I know I have, a sweet hope of glory in my

204

soul," sang Ganty, who had not been told.

After the event, some of the UDC put it around that they had simply forgotten about Ganty during all the business of approving plans for the extension to the council-house estate, of inviting tenders and reading the surveyors' reports on contractors' bids. Ganty Pugh paid no rates, was on no electoral roll, it wasn't reasonable to expect the UDC to have him constantly in its thoughts. As it was, the contracting firm and its workforce were from Up the Line, as the town still said despite Dr Beeching, and were totally ignorant of Ganty's existence. When the men with the theodolites and red-and-white poles turned up one morning and started to cover the Common Hills in a criss-cross pattern of stakes and white tape, Ganty's reaction was to slip off and lie low for a few days. When he returned, the bulldozer and sledgehammers had started work and the air-raid shelter was no more than a pile of broken bricks. When the navvy ganger opened the site up at eight in the morning, he found Ganty sitting slumped on the rubble, silent, eyes shut, though not asleep. There was no way of knowing how long he had been there.

"Wouldn't speak, nor move, nor nothing, Sergeant," said John Hughes. "Had to carry him into the hut in the finish. Might have been deaf and blind for all the notice he took. Carmarthen, of course. Awful place, that. Put my uncle Billy Bowman in Carmarthen, and he was all right really, just getting on a bit and forgetting himself, only he never could abide rice pudding. And that nosey old cow next door wouldn't leave him alone ever since his wife died, and she kept bringing him round these bowls of rice pudding. And he couldn't bring himself to tell her straight out after she'd took the trouble, so he used to take them out the back and empty them over the wall into her yard. And the old bugger went and reported him, and they committed him into Carmarthen. Went to visit him once after he'd been in there a couple of months with all them old Napoleons and Jungle Jims and whatnots, and he wasn't the same man at all. Just sat round snivelling the whole time. Awful place. But that's where they'll put him, sure as eggs." "None of our business," said Waldo Persimmon Walters. The town, never having claimed Ganty for one of its own, now lost him for good.

For the first few weeks in the hospital, Ganty was little better than a vegetable. Awake, he was technically conscious while seeming quite unaware of his surroundings. Then, very gradually at first, the staff began to notice improvements. He appeared to register what was going on around him for longer and longer periods. Little by little, he started first to sit up in bed and then to co-operate with the physiotherapist. Soon he was up and about for longer each day, until he could eventually be trusted to feed himself and go to the bathroom unaided. Occasionally his face flickered in a weak smile, but his unfocused eyes were about as expressive as virgin blotting-paper, and he never again spoke. His monologue was over. The staff liked him because he would sit quietly and obey without fuss when spoken to. "Blood will out," Nurse Huw Pugh, no relation, was fond of saying, "Proper little old gentleman, our Mr Pugh. Conversation a bit lacking, mind." As the months and years passed, a subtle change took place in Ganty's severely limited vocabulary of posture and gesture. Defeat blurred slowly into resignation, resignation in turn into something very like contentment, but it was all far too gradual to be noticed by the nurses who saw him every day. It never occurred to them that only now had he finally dared to believe they were going to let him stay. They never paused to reflect that for twenty years nobody had willingly touched Ganty Pugh or shared a roof with him, while now, suddenly, as Ganty measured things, people touched him all the time, spoke more or less kindly to him, kept him out of the bloody scummy old weather in a real bed. They never imagined that, after twenty years, Ganty Pugh was home, or that he told nobody about it for fear the spell might break.

"There you are, Mr Pugh, I'll just plump up these pillows

and you can sit nice and quiet till it's time for tea," said Huw Pugh, no relation, on the afternoon before Ganty died in his sleep. The ward was quiet, and Huw decided to risk leaving them unsupervised for a few minutes while he fetched his library book from his locker. At the door, he was stopped in his tracks by an unfamiliar sound. Ganty had started to sing.

"If Johnny he was here this night he'd save me from all harm,
But he's cruising the Atlantic on board the Unicorn. . . ."

The nurse turned to look back. The old man hadn't moved; his eyes were still blank.

". . . He's a lion bold in battle, all foes he doth destroy
Like some royal king of honour all upon the banks of Troy."

Ganty fell silent. One of his rare smiles flitted across his face. The late-afternoon sun passed briefly between two clouds and the round stained-glass insert in the ward window bathed his pillows in a wash of emerald, blue, scarlet and gold. For a few long moments, he was as gorgeous and irreproachable as a peacock.

Question Marks

A famous writer died, honoured and full of years.

As is customary on these occasions, the obituaries had been drafted many years in advance and in most cases required little or no amendment before publication. In many instances, all that happened was a brief confirmatory telephone call from editorial assistant to author. In a few cases, circumstances prevented even this simple precaution. As is customary on these occasions, and especially so when the deceased has achieved worldwide fame, the overall tone of the obituaries was respectful, dignified, affirmative, taking for granted the reader's awareness of and assent to the worth of the dead man's works, mentioning any limitations only where doing so helped to define the nature of his writings, never so as to belittle their quality. Indeed, in some cases the tenor of the obituaries went a little beyond the bounds of conventional lapidary praise. Eminent critics who had been less than fully committed to the writer's cause during his life seemed to have had their reservations annulled by his death, and celebrated what they had hitherto somewhat diffidently acknowledged.

The writer's country gave him a solemn and spectacular state funeral. It was a vast South American state, a nominal republic ruled, as far as that was ever practicable, by its own military. The land was as various as it was extensive: vertiginous mountain peaks in the west, enormous grassland plains in the interior, near-tropical forest in the north, a cold wet rocky desert in the far south, a handful of small and gracious ex-colonial cities on the east coast, each besieged by an ever-growing investment of fetid slums. The country's natural resources were nearly bottomless, it exported food and minerals to half the civilized world, and large numbers of its own citizens lived out their days in extreme poverty, many of them the alternate victims and perpetrators of violent crime. The country's landed and professional classes had a long and proud tradition of the highest conceivable literary and cultural aspirations, while most of the population had never read the dead writer's stories and many could not read at all. It was at least as ridiculous as any other country in the world and more so than some.

One of the writer's ancestors had played a prominent part in the ferocious and complex series of early nineteenth-century military actions which the country nowadays called the Liberation, but which would always remain for the foreigner, especially one from the northern hemisphere, a hopelessly confused and tragicomic exercise in bloody futility. The writer himself, however, eschewed all involvement in national or international politics. On the few occasions when he was taken off guard and refusal to answer a public question would itself have been a species of comment, his political utterances were gnomic to the point of mockery. Successive governments regarded him none the less with deep ambivalence. He was at one and the same time the cherished symbol of the nation's intellectual achievements and, like all intellectuals, a potential threat. He had, moreover, an established and highly influential international following, so that had it ever become necessary to silence him, there would have been difficulties. Furthermore, if there is anything governments mistrust more than what they may not be able to control, it is anything they do not understand, and to successive governments this writer's books remained closed ones. Dead, the writer was in one sense a great loss, but also became both useful and safe. The solemn renaming of the National Library as his permanent memorial, the lying-in-state in the old cathedral high on the cliffs, the funeral procession taking two hours to pass at the slow-march were all unifying, cathartic and diverting. They also meant that, at last, the government could rest assured that the writer would never talk out of turn. The ceremonial burial, incidentally, was in direct defiance of the writer's express wishes. With characteristic ambiguity, he had also said he would not be surprised if his wishes were disregarded.

If the relief tempering the government's regret had been barely detectable in the obituaries, it was far easier to discern it in the more leisurely critical reappraisals of the writer and his works which now, as is customary, began to appear. Not that the critical community suffered any real change of heart; their man had already been the subject of far too many learned treatises for that to happen credibly. He had been too long on the university reading-list and even the secondary-school syllabus for there to be any surprise insights left. It was more a question of emphasis; a matter of the tone of voice.

The writer had not been prolific for one who lived so long and began publishing so young, and had always remained something of a miniaturist in form. He now seemed to exercise a posthumous osmotic influence on the writing of his critics, and the new retrospective reviews were refreshingly brief. Nearly all began with fairly standard appraisals of his early work, the short stories of violent and primitive pampas life in the previous century written as vivacious parodies of the better Wild West fictions of the period, his "gauchos and indios" work, as he had once called it. Similar treatment was afforded to the roughly equivalent slumland gangster stories written at about the same time. All of this criticism could just as easily have been written ten or even twenty years earlier, although it was noticeable that none of the critics chose to perpetuate the writer's own mild refusal to see these stories as anything more than reasonably competent entertainments. The real difference appeared when the reviewers moved on to the mature works of his middle and old age.

Question Marks

At the time of writing, in fact, these early stories had brought him little enough acclaim, and virtually none outside his native land. This had never seemed to discourage him in the slightest. His family circumstances left him financially comfortable, and it was doubtful that he even needed his salary as Director of the library which would one day bear his name. He was a true amateur of literature. One of his small circle in those early and middle years before the spread of his fame claimed that the man would have continued to write even if there were no hope of his finding a single reader, let alone a publisher.

It was conventional wisdom among reviewers of the later works that the writer seemed to have read and remembered every single book in that national library. His erudition was startling in its breadth, if not quite so impressive in its depth. His mature pieces were liable to quote authoritatively, though quite unpretentiously, from sources in any of thirty-two living and five dead languages, with dates separated by centuries or millennia, on subjects ranging from thaumaturgy through steam engines to jurisprudence. What was unconventional about what the critics now wrote about these pieces was the almost total absence of question marks.

One of the writer's least reverent academic admirers had many years previously claimed, humorously, to be able to identify as such any review of the writer solely by means of its high incidence of question marks. It was true that the characteristic posture adopted by his critics seemed to entail frequent use of stock phrases like "can it be, I wonder . . .?" or "is he, one cannot resist asking, really telling us . . . ?" Part of the reason for this was transparent and perfectly commonplace. In many of his fictions and essays, the writer set out quite overtly to provoke questions in the reader's mind. The writer was conventionally held to be concerned with, *inter alia*, the opaque, arbitrary and quite ineffable nature of time, the absurdity of fiction's use of lies to tell truths, the fatal beauty of the impregnable paradox, man's baffling insistence that the universe is somehow purposeful, the impossible incompleteness of the infinite set. He provoked the reader's questions on these and other matters in a prose usually ironic, always lucid, economical, learnedly demotic. Its only extravagant quality was the almost total effectiveness with which it could be translated into any language where it might conceivably find a readership. His forms included the truncated metaphysical squib, eerie fantasies offered as realistic naturalism, haunting and totally inhuman pseudomythologies, multi-level philosophical and psychological puzzles masquerading as detective or adventure fiction. One critic had remarked that the writer's underlying intent seemed to be not so much the pulling of the metaphorical rug from under the reader as to prompt the reader to ask on his own initiative: What rug? More than one confessed, not entirely facetiously, that prolonged reading of his works left them with the uncomfortable conviction that the writer had, at some earlier date, already scripted the whole of creation and subsequent events and had now moved on to more interesting matters.

Another reason for the reviewers' question marks was less easily detected, however. As one commentator wrote, either the writer's life had been completely uneventful, or someone (the writer?) had ruthlessly eliminated all evidence to the contrary. He did not marry, he formed few friendships and no close ones, he wrote, he administered his beloved library, he occasionally lectured, but otherwise—nothing. He was even almost indecently healthy, although in old age he grew increasingly blind. There was, however, one intriguing exception to this, even if it was supported by little more than rumour. When the writer was in his late teens, the capital city which was his lifelong home was plagued for two or three months by a series of bizarre and utterly pointless practical jokes. Expensively produced posters appeared overnight, announcing a public concert of entirely imaginary symphonic works on a date just over ten years in the past. A neatly stacked pile of new and scarce imported housebricks was left in the forecourt of the State Legislature, one of them bearing an adhesive label addressed in accomplished calligraphy to the Minister for Culture, a non-existent post. When dawn broke one morning on the thirty stately lampposts in the Avenue of the Liberation, all but one of them wore gigantic black silk opera hats. The exception wore an outsize ermine glove. Other events followed almost daily. The populace assumed the many strikingly futile public gestures of that summer to be jokes, although they made nobody laugh. There were persistent rumours at the time that the young writer was the author, though not the executant, of these outlandish pranks. The rumours never entirely died out, not least because the writer always politely but absolutely refused to comment on the subject. No doubt these rumours played their part in sowing tiny seeds of doubt as to whether the mind of the great man was always entirely serious.

Certainly he did nothing to dispel such doubts himself. His later publications were larded with pieces which caused reviewers' eyebrows to be raised a little, each raising reflected later as a question mark in a review. In one story, a multimillionaire obsessed by the study and compilation of indices renounced his worldly affairs to devote himself to compiling the Ultimate Index of all words ever written anywhere in any language. Dying with his task incomplete, he was nevertheless still wealthy enough to fund in perpetuity a trust charged with first completing and constantly updating the Ultimate Index, then providing the Ultimate Index with its own sub-index (which, of course, would entail consequent expansion of the Ultimate Index itself which in turn, depending upon pagination, might mean further expansion of the sub-index, and so on), then with providing the sub-index with its own sub-index, and so forth. This piece might well have been less delicately treated had it come from an unknown writer. As it was, most commentators paused barely long enough to raise eyebrows and question marks before passing on to the next item in the collection. There were many similar examples.

The writer's personal behaviour in later life, and particularly his notorious refusal to be drawn on the meaning of his works, was a further source of unease for some of his more solemn critical advocates. After his lionization in his middle fifties, he was in constant demand in Europe and America. He rarely accepted such invitations as the years wore on, and was unfailingly dignified and courteous when he did, but he nevertheless usually managed to unsettle any admirers rash enough to air their own interpretations of his books in his presence. "Ah," he would say after following, with the expression of a sinner receiving divine enlightenment, the earnest exposition of each literary editor or campus zealot, "Ah," the long upper lip almost impeccably stiff, the large brown purblind eye gleaming softly, "So *that* is what I meant!" Some critics began to have an uneasy feeling that each of the infrequent collections was a test set them by the author to see if they could tell his sheep from his goats, to discover whether their personal public commitment to the "greatness" or "significance" of similar earlier pieces was strong enough to overcome their objective judgement. Reviewers discreetly refrained from asserting that there were at least six equally valid explanations for the extraordinary expression on the face of the corpse of the king to whom, on the royal deathbed, God had secretly revealed the (unrevealed to the reader) true purpose of Life, and instead wondered whether, perhaps, there might possibly be several?

The old man's death put a stop to all this. The excess question marks died with him because the reviewers were no longer looking over their shoulders to try to see if he was laughing at them. In their relief, they were probably kinder to him than he deserved. At any rate, his reputation did not suffer the eclipse, partial or total, which so often follows an artist's death. One writer even had the wit and grace to wonder publicly whether the deceased had planned things thus. The epithet "great" looked firmly fixed in place.

Question Marks

The dead man's literary executor was his former assistant and successor as Director of the library, a brilliant young man whom the writer had dubbed his "proxy grandson". The will contained no instructions beyond the location of the key to the author's inner sanctum, a small room off the Director's main office suite where he had done all his writing. Nobody else had entered it during his lifetime except the personal secretary to whom he had been forced to dictate following his loss of sight, an elderly lady who survived him by less than a month. It had originally been a dressing-room when the building was erected as a colonial governor's palace. When the young Director opened it up, he found it to contain a government-issue clerk's desk of obsolete design for which no keys could be traced, an expensive new revolving chair, pneumatically adjustable in height and rake, a gilt-framed full-length tailor's mirror, an old and crude wooden lectern on which lay a dog-eared A4 sketchpad filled with dozens of incompetent self-portraits in charcoal, and twelve standard four-drawer filing cabinets. The cabinets proved to be stuffed to bursting-point with thousands of the writer's work-sheets, his neat penmanship in many cases rendered almost illegible by amendments, crossings out, transpositions and comments executed in red crayon to distinguish them from the black ink of the draft text proper. The number and content of the work-sheets showed clearly that the author's practice had been to draft and redraft each individual piece perhaps dozens of times before he was satisfied with it. Their apparently total disorder suggested either a complete lack of system in their storage, or that the writer's system was so arcane that it would be quicker to start from scratch then to try to unravel it. The Director let it be known that the deceased had left a treasure-trove of manuscript material for future research, but that a Herculean task of sortation and classification must first be completed before the world's scholars could sensibly be given access to it.

The Director's other duties permitted him to devote only a

little of his time to this task, so he set about recruiting an assistant from among his students for, like his predecessor, he also held a fairly undemanding Chair at the local university. His choice fell upon a Texan postgraduate researcher, a huge young man whose menacing and simian appearance was quite at odds with his agile mind, his gentle sense of humour and the fact that his voice had never broken. The Director engaged him after listening with mounting amusement to his deadpan account of his experiences when, while working his way through college, he had been part of a team of temporary workers trying to reassemble several hundred thousand cheque forms which a bank employee had inadvertently put through the high-speed shredder before they had been brought to account.

Initially, the task looked truly daunting and the Texan's quiet cheerfulness did much to keep the Director from despair. Progress was still painfully slow several months later, and by now even the Texan was beginning to sound weary. Then, just as the Director was about to summon his young assistant to discuss whether they should not be realistic and delegate the work to one of the wealthy computer-backed American faculties known to be avid for the honour, the Texan put his head out of the inner sanctum and asked if he could spare a few minutes.

The Director seated the young man on the sofa and paced up and down his strip of carpet, as was his habit during interviews. He was intrigued to note signs of both puzzlement and excitement in the falsetto drawl. With obvious restraint, his massive young assistant outlined his progress so far. He had, he said, thus far managed to identify some three hundred work-sheets as belonging to one or other of twenty individual pieces, and had even established a tentative chronological order for the sheets of one piece. He had proved by patient trial and error that the red crayon comments, as well as being well nigh incomprehensible to him, were a positive hindrance to this sortation process and he now ignored them. However, he was much less dejected about their slow progress for two reasons.

Firstly, only twelve out of the twenty pieces were in Spanish or English, the languages in which the writer had exclusively published. He could read most of the others with varying degrees of difficulty, but in two cases he could not even identify the kind of script, never mind the language. He had been forced with these two to regard the writing as meaningless visual patterns, which made sortation as laborious as it was unreliable. In the second place, he had not been able to relate any of the pieces, not even those where he was sure he had something close to the final text, to any of the published works. If they were dealing with unknown texts while supposing the exact opposite, he said, it was small wonder they had found it such hard going at first. The Director froze in mid-stride, slowly lowered his raised foot to the carpet, thought for a moment then wheeled abruptly towards the open door and called to an aide to summon a locksmith.

In the right-hand drawer of the clerk's desk, they found three pristine box files. These contained the fair manuscript copies of exactly one hundred numbered pieces in thirty-two living and five dead languages. All were unpublished. Each manuscript was meticulously initialled and dated. It was noticeable that the numerical order was widely different from the chronological one. The very last one, dictated to his confidential secretary a few days before the author's death, was number twelve. The earliest, dated one year after his appointment to the library over half a century earlier, was number eighty-four. Incredibly, sixty of the pieces appeared to have been completed within ten days of each other at a point roughly midway between these two extremes. The Director and the Texan tried to establish some connection between the manuscript dates and those of the published works and failed. The nearest they could get to any sort of correspondence was that the first English translation of the major collection which had first established his international reputation (America, of course, had led the way) had appeared almost exactly two years after the date of the 'incredible sixty'.

Robert Sproat

With definitive texts to work backwards from, the young American completed his labours on the work-sheets in a matter of months, leaving for subsequent specialists the pleasure of wrangling over the exact order of the various redrafts, especially in the more obscure languages. During the course of his work, he noticed that most of the 'incredible sixty' pieces had been the subject of truly enormous numbers of redrafts. He suggested that this showed the author to have been working on them more or less in parallel over a very long period of time, until some circumstance enabled him to put the finishing touches to all of them. Neither he nor the Director could even conjecture what that circumstance might have been, since the content of the forty-two out of the sixty that they could read between them ran the whole gamut of the author's very considerable range, making it difficult to see anything that all or even many of them had in common besides authorship.

The Director now found himself in something of a quandary. It had all along been his intention that the sorted and classified work-sheets should be fully available to scholarly researchers. He had no qualms about extending this availability to the hundred fair copies, and could also envisage their publication purely as academic research material. What worried him was their possible publication as works of literature in their own right. Those that were in languages he could read seemed to him to be of very high quality, yet his dead friend and mentor had chosen not to publish them during his lifetime. Did he consider them unworthy to bear his name publicly? Would publication now harm his posthumous reputation? (Even in his grave, noted the young Director, the old man pushed up question marks.) On an impulse, the Director had earlier had one of the childish self-portraits mounted and framed. It stood now on his desk beside the last official portrait, executed by a titled English photographer in the writer's blind old age. The blind eye of the photograph now focused sharply on the Director's own, while the sighted one of the crude sketch refused to acknowledge his existence. Neither offered him any help. At length the Director decided to publish piece number twelve, the last one written, telling himself without real conviction that the author had died before he had time to make any final decision about it.

The story duly appeared and caused quite a stir. The news of the writer's bequest and the Director's dilemma was common knowledge in literary circles and the publication had been eagerly awaited. Unusually for such a short piece in such a low-circulation magazine (the Director had deliberately chosen a rather staid academic quarterly to avoid any suggestion of sensationalism), the story was discussed at some length in literary publications and even some of the better-quality dailies. It was adjudged a typical piece of near-vintage quality. It was a witty and world-weary lecture delivered to a class of trainee intelligence agents at a government spy school by a seasoned field operative. Its point, in whose direction the lecturer attempted to nudge his pupils by means of a series of ever more convoluted and hilarious examples, was that the process, so beloved of thriller-writers, of trying to establish the number of levels of bluff in operation in a given confrontation is in fact as pointless as it is enervating, since all you need to know is the oddness or evenness of that number. A tossed coin has a fifty-fifty chance of getting this right. Some reviewers claimed, with a good deal of justification, to detect a strong vein of self-parody. Others mentioned the occasional allusion which came dangerously close to pretension, or a straining for an effect never quite achieved, but these were seen as only minor flaws. The old man's reluctance to publish was held to be, just, understandable, but the consensus was that he was being too much of a perfectionist. Letters to editors appeared over respected signatures urging publication of the other ninety-nine stories if they were of comparable quality. The nationalistic elements of the popular media decided that here was an honourable patriotic (and newsworthy) cause, and promoted it accordingly. The government stepped in. A memorial edition of the one hundred stories was decreed, to be published simultaneously in Spanish and English. The young Director was appointed as its editor and given an indefinite sabbatical from his other duties.

The young man was greatly relieved to find that he had not harmed his dead professor's reputation. He set about translating personally those pieces in languages he knew and farming out the rest to selected specialists. In order to maintain public interest in the project, the publishers insisted that a few individual stories should in the meantime appear in selected periodicals. With the publication of each story, the critical response repeated itself, became more confident, more clearly defined. It also brought about a still further reappraisal of the work published in the writer's lifetime. If the great writer had reservations about publishing such marvellous stories, ran the new conventional wisdom, should we not be doubly appreciative of the pieces he judged worthy to bear his name in public? Nobody, as it happened, wondered publicly whether the dead man had planned things thus.

Relieved though he was by all this, the Director could never completely shake off his nagging doubts about what he was doing. Although the reviewers increasingly mentioned the slight shortcomings of the newly published stories only as a matter of cursory formality before turning to praise, he himself could not help noticing that he felt the same small misgivings about every single one of the hundred stories as it became possible for him to read them. This puzzled and worried him. He experienced nothing like it when reading the works published before his mentor's death, this conviction that each story was not quite conveying to him the writer's full intent. The other question marks refused to lie down. Why had his friend numbered the hundred stories in such idiosyncratic fashion? Why had he preserved all the work-sheets for them but none, seemingly, for the published works? Why had he never published even one of them?

On the day he received the final translations from the Cornell and Aberdeen professors to whom they had been entrusted, the Director sat in his office brooding on these questions. As had become his habit, he gazed, barely focusing, at the two portraits of his friend on his desk. He noticed, for perhaps the twentieth time, that the dead man had initialled his charcoal drawing in red crayon, but on this occasion it immediately occurred to him that nobody had yet had the chance to make any systematic study of the cryptic red-crayon comments on the work-sheets. No sooner had he thought this than the sudden memory of two of the more striking comments sent him running into the former dressing-room.

Using the lumbering Texan's improbably neat indexing system, he located in minutes what, without it, might have taken him weeks. His memory of the two terse comments confirmed, he consulted the index again and extracted for comparison first another three work-sheets then, hardly glancing at the index, a further ten. The old clerk's desk was soon covered with growing piles of work-sheets and the Director's own notes. An hour later, he emerged into the main office, waved his lunch away untouched and proceeded to do what had been impossible for him until that morning.

He sat at his own desk and read all one hundred stories straight through in the numerical order assigned them by their author. As soon as he finished, he repeated the process, except this time he reverted to the original manuscript rather than the translation wherever this was possible for him. Having done this, he sat back and stared at the twin portraits with a dazed mixture of awe, disbelief and joy on his face.

The one hundred stories now stood revealed to him as an interrelated whole. As well as being a self-contained piece, each contained a number of references to other stories. A few contained allusions to every one of the other ninety-nine. Some allusions were overt quotations or other direct references, more were oblique and subtle, each a tiny brilliancy in itself. Often they worked on more than one level; a cross-reference in a late story operating in a way which revealed to the reader for the first time other allusions missed at first reading in earlier stories, sometimes with the allusions thus revealed themselves in turn illuminating still earlier missed references. Reading the stories in order brought these allusions to light in ever greater numbers, revealing more and more of the complexity and beauty of the interlinking pattern, filling the reader with an ever-growing sense of wonder. Moreover, stunned and uplifted though the Director's reading had left him, he was convinced that still further insights were denied him because many of the allusions were dependent on the translation process for their effect (as when, to take a simple example, an invading warlord in a story written in his own language took a captured serf's comment to be a mispronounced compliment in that language, whereas a later story in modern English suggested indirectly that it could equally well have been a mispronounced insult in the serf's own tongue). The one hundred stories were in effect one great book intended for a readership fluent in thirty-two living and five dead languages. The writer never published it because he barely managed to complete it before dying. Hence the vast quantity of work-sheets and the need to retain them for cross-reference—a small drafting change in one piece might have ramifications for one or even all of the others. There was no such need in the case of the published works, since the author had at some stage in writing each of them concluded that it would never form part of his noble structure. The one hundred stories were the real work of the great man's creative life. The published works, so admired by the world, were his rejects. The expression on the Director's face was truly extraordinary as he reflected that the writer's real thoughts on the world's opinion of him were a secret which would share forever his unwanted and unsurprising monumental tomb.

Acknowledgements

Acknowledgements are due to the following publications in which some of the stories in this volume made their first appearance: Anne Devlin, "Passages", *Threshold*, no. 32, Winter 1982, and "The Journey to Somewhere Else", *Irish Press*, 20 March 1982; Ronald Frame, "Secrets", *Punch*, 4 November 1981; Rachel Gould, "Mrs Elizabeth Davies", *Vogue*, September 1982; Helen Harris, "The Lizard behind the Lavatory Cistern", *London Magazine*, November 1981; Robert Sproat, "Stunning the Punters", *Fiction Magazine*, vol. 1, no. 4 Winter 1982.